THE HEART ALWAYS KNOWS

THE HEART ALWAYS KNOWS

ESTRELLITA H. REDMON, MD

Tampa, Florida

This book is a work of fiction. The names, characters and events in this book are the products of the author's imagination or are used fictitiously. Any similarity to real persons living or dead is coincidental and not intended by the author.

The views and opinions expressed in this book are solely those of the author and do not reflect the views or opinions of Gatekeeper Press. Gatekeeper Press is not to be held responsible for and expressly disclaims responsibility of the content herein.

The Heart Always Knows

Published by Gatekeeper Press
7853 Gunn Hwy, Suite 209
Tampa, FL 33626
www.GatekeeperPress.com

Copyright © 2022 by Estrellita H. Redmon, MD
All rights reserved. Neither this book, nor any parts within it may be sold or reproduced in any form or by any electronic or mechanical means, including information storage and retrieval systems, without permission in writing from the author. The only exception is by a reviewer, who may quote short excerpts in a review.

Library of Congress Control Number: 2022946028

ISBN (hardcover): 9781662933042
ISBN (paperback): 9781662933059
eISBN: 9781662933066

*This book is dedicated to my loving husband,
Gregory S. Redmon, Esq., who continues to encourage me
in my medical career and writing pursuits.*

CONTENTS

ABOUT THE BOOK ix
CHAPTER 1 1
CHAPTER 2 11
CHAPTER 3 24
CHAPTER 4 31
CHAPTER 5 41
CHAPTER 6 49
CHAPTER 7 55
CHAPTER 8 59
CHAPTER 9 66
CHAPTER 10 75
CHAPTER 11 82
CHAPTER 12 93
CHAPTER 13 101
EPILOGUE 107
REFERENCES 109
ABOUT THE AUTHOR 110

ABOUT THE BOOK

When I started the draft for this book in 2017, my timetable for completing it was two years. Little did I know that it would take me over five years to complete the work. The challenges included personal health issues in 2018, resulting in the need for visual and neurological treatments that would last for over two years.

Just when I thought I was back on the writing path, the world was faced with the COVID-19 pandemic. I found myself, as a physician executive, thrust into a healthcare crisis that was unimaginable prior to March 2020. We continue to deal with the results of the pandemic, even as this book is finally completed. The crisis of access to health care in rural and non-urban towns in America and the disparities that exist were highlighted as COVID-19 infections and deaths spread across our nation and efforts were made to develop a vaccine as quickly and as safely as possible. While mass vaccinations started in December 2020 in the United States, many citizens of rural towns would remain unvaccinated, due either to social determinants preventing them from having access or continued vaccine hesitancy and resistance.

While this is a fictional novel and the town of Sienna is fictional, it is based on the great insight I received from Dr. Pat Munroe Woodward and his wife, Mrs. Mary Jane May Woodward, in June 2017. Spending time with them and hearing their stories of private practice in a rural town gave me inspiration to continue to move forward with the book as well as to change the main character to a pediatric physician instead of a family medicine physician. Words are inadequate to thank them enough for their time and patience. I also had the immense pleasure to meet and interview Mrs. Betty Jones Dawson, who served as Dr. Woodward's dedicated nurse for over two decades.

My brother, Dr. Enrique Howard, who chose to have a dental practice in the same town where Dr. Woodward practiced, gave me additional insight into the life and role of dentistry in rural America. Improving access to preventative dental treatment and acute dental services, outside of the emergency room, for those most vulnerable is a great public health need throughout small towns in America.

All references to patients and incidents are fictional and are not true encounters. While there are places, universities, and names of cities and towns that exist in reality, none are truly associated with the events of the book.

I must acknowledge my husband, Gregory S. Redmon, whose love and support continues to encourage me to write. I must also give thanks to my parents, Edward W. Howard (deceased) and Margie M. Howard, who stressed the importance of education and allowed me to pursue my dream of becoming a physician.

Our family continues to grow, and education continues to remain in the forefront of our pursuits. Thank you to my son, Victor G. Redmon, MD, and my daughter, Carissa Redmon Battle, MD, for answering the call and becoming physicians. Thank you to their devoted spouses, Danielle Jones Redmon and Lawrence J. Battle, for standing by them despite the long hours they spend away from home to take care of patients. Thank you to my grandson, Samuel V. Redmon, for the joy he brings to our lives.

For all who read this book, I hope you find it rewarding and encouraging. I have profound respect for physicians, dentists, and allied health care professionals who choose to practice in a rural setting. May the Lord bless and keep each of you!

CHAPTER 1

*"The steps of a good man are ordered by the Lord:
and he delighteth in his way."*
(Psalm 37:23 KJV)[1]

Dr. Steven Hamilton stared out the window of his small office as he thought about the last patient he had seen, Sabrina Bartley. Sabrina was a sweet two-year-old toddler and the only child of Carrie Ellis Bartley, who had lost her husband to leukemia when Sabrina was just over a year old. It was now April 1968, and Valium had only been on the market since November 1963, but Steve's wife, Alice, had told him it was considered a "wonder drug" by the ladies in the town's bridge club. "Doc" (as he was referred to by most in the town) knew that Carrie was on Valium; she had told him how much she needed it to deal with the deep loss and anxiety she continued to experience since the death of her husband, Austin. Carrie worked in her family's funeral home, and it wasn't the best job for her, given her emotional struggles. Ellis Funeral Home and Mortuary was a multigenerational business and the only Black-owned funeral home in Sienna. Doc was a pediatrician, and yet he still discussed Carrie's job with her, although he knew that it might not change what she did since it was the only occupation she knew. Carrie wasn't the type of person to venture out beyond her comfort zone, and all he could hope for was to give little Sabrina good medical care and to pray for Carrie and the family.

Nestled in the northwestern part of Florida, Sienna had a population of around 17,800, which was almost twice as many people as when Doc was growing up in the small town. After high school he left for college and graduated from Davidson College in North Carolina and then headed to Georgia for medical school at Emory. Wisdom would have dictated that he not return to such a small town, especially given the opportunities that existed for pediatrics in Atlanta and other larger cities. He had been warned by several of the teaching physicians, called "attendings," at the University of Florida that it was nearly impossible to have a successful pediatric practice in a rural town and the odds for success were very slim. But Alice had convinced him that it was right for him to return home because the other two general practitioners in town were well into their late sixties and the town needed a young, well-trained pediatrician. Along with Alice, Doc's father had pleaded with him to return home where starting and growing a practice would be easier, given the family ties to the town.

Doc had acquired a loan to start his practice, and it was a friend of the family, George Williamson, who had placed the bid for $7,500 and made the initial down payment to hold the building. It was quite a deal, considering the Jefferson Street location. Doc and his father spent time remodeling the place, which had previously been a restaurant. The amount of the loan was enough to cover the furnishings and medical equipment, and over the last year the practice had grown substantially.

Doc's parents, Lloyd and Martha Hamilton, had come to Sienna in 1934 from southwest Georgia and purchased a hundred acres of land for a nominal price. Within five years, they had a sustainable farm and acquired an additional five hundred acres, along with an influx of workers, both Black and White. The Hamiltons weren't considered rich by most, but they were well-off enough to have influence in the town.

Lloyd had grown up in a very poor family and had seen his father treated poorly by those who earned higher incomes, but the

Black residents and workers were treated even worse in southwest Georgia. Lloyd had witnessed beatings of Black folks, and he could think of no good reason for any human being to be treated that way. The Ku Klux Klan was very prominent in that area, and Lloyd had made a promise to himself that he would never treat or talk to others the way his family was treated, or the even worse way he had seen the Black people treated.

Thus, he used his influence to treat the workers on his farm with equal respect, regardless of whether they were White or a person of color. If the workers didn't respond to verbal instruction and correction, then Lloyd would fire them and move on to hiring someone else who might value working for him more. No one in town harassed Lloyd about his equal treatment of the workers, probably because they never knew when they might need to borrow money from him.

George Williamson, on the other hand, had real fortune from the profits he made in the stock market, investing in Coca-Cola early in the history of the company. He was a Coca-Cola millionaire and the owner and president of First Sienna Bank. Despite George's wealth, he appeared to most as a simple and common man. Only the locals knew that he was probably the richest man within a hundred miles.

"Doc? I finished cleaning the last exam room, and the front door is locked."

Doc turned around and saw Betsy standing in the doorway. At five-foot-four and average weight, she had a pleasant face with blond hair that complemented her blue eyes. Betsy was loved by the patients and their parents, not because she was soft with them but because her compassion was obvious. Doc was glad to have Betsy around as his nurse.

"Thanks, Betsy. It was busy today, wasn't it?" Doc continued before she could respond. "Go home and get some rest. Thanks again."

"Glad to do it, Doc. Good night."

Doc entered the far back room that served as his private office and finished writing notes on the last two patients he had seen.

Then he locked up the office and walked the two blocks to his home off Broadway Street. It was a two-story brick home with a nice large wraparound front porch and double oak doors at the front entrance. The four-bedroom, two-bath house was the right size for his family. Alice and the three boys spent a lot of time together without him, given the long hours he devoted to his patients, both in the office and the hospital.

Approaching the front door, he could smell the aroma of roast chicken, and as he opened the door Alice walked toward him from the kitchen.

"Hi, honey. It's good to have you home, and it's still early!" Alice hugged him as he returned the hug and kissed her gently on the lips. She took his hat and hung it on the coat rack by the door, and the two walked into the kitchen together, hand in hand.

They were both raised together in the church, and their first real connection as a couple occurred at a youth retreat in Carrabelle Beach, the year they turned fourteen. Attending high school together in Sienna, they spent time at the First Presbyterian Church in Bible studies and summer youth retreats. After high school, they left Sienna and went to separate colleges. Alice attended Converse College in Spartanburg, South Carolina, and Doc attended Davidson College in Charlotte, North Carolina, so they were about ninety miles apart. Nevertheless, Doc was committed to maintaining the relationship with frequent commutes to Spartanburg.

After graduation in 1958, Doc headed to Emory for medical school, and Alice taught in a school for deaf children in Dallas for a year. A year later they were married, and by the time Doc graduated from medical school in 1962, their first son, Steven Hamilton Jr., was born. He was followed by two other sons: Marcus in 1964 and Phillip in 1966. Now Alice was pregnant and due to deliver their fourth child sometime in October.

"Yeah, it's good to be home early. I didn't have any patients to see at the hospital, and the cases today in the office were not complex."

"Well that's good. I played bridge today, and—oh, I almost forgot—Wilma called and said she couldn't stop by your office after work because she became ill today. I think she even had a fever, as well as a really bad cough. Anyway, I told her I'd let you know."

"Daddy, Daddy!" Steve ran around the corner and hugged his daddy, followed by Marcus, who laughed as Doc picked him up and spun him around. The three headed to the dining room for dinner. Alice had already placed Phillip in his high chair with a small amount of food on the tray.

Finishing up the conversation about Wilma, Doc commented on how a respiratory viral infection was spreading around, and he hoped Wilma wouldn't be sick for too long. They finished up dinner and the boys were put to bed, and after cleaning up the kitchen, the couple settled down to watch TV for a couple of hours. But it wasn't long before Doc fell asleep on the couch. He had been up since before 4 a.m., when the emergency room had called him to come in and evaluate a three-year-old with a rash and high fever. This was the life of a solo pediatrician in a small town.

* * *

Wilma Washington Hinson entered her house just after twelve noon. She felt guilty that she couldn't stay at work at the hospital or stop by Doc's office, but it was for the best that she had left work early. It was all she could do to get home before a wave of nausea and then vomiting occurred. She had made it to the bathroom just in time to vomit in the toilet. She located the can of ginger ale she had seen in the back of the refrigerator, opened it, and took a couple of sips; then she undressed, put on her nightgown, and within a few minutes of lying on the bed, she fell asleep.

Wilma was born in 1940 to Henry and Alma Washington, who had moved from northern Georgia to Sienna in hopes of finding stable work in the late 1930s and fleeing the oppressive treatment of Blacks in the northern Georgia town. The Washingtons had heard that the town of Sienna had many Blacks who were doing much better than most Blacks in northern Georgia.

They met Lloyd Hamilton shortly after arriving in Sienna and were hired immediately as field hands. Both Henry and Alma were steady and responsible workers and showed creativity toward improving the productivity of the crops. Lloyd took notice of the quality of their work. After many years of working in the fields, Alma was moved to working inside the home for Martha, and Henry became one of the foremen.

The Washingtons only had two children, Malcolm and Wilma. Malcolm was born in 1936, the same year as Doc, and Wilma was born four years later. In Doc's family, there were six Hamilton children; the two oldest were boys and the younger four were girls.

Despite the challenges that occurred in the small town, the two sets of children, from two different races, grew up together and played together. The Washingtons built their home on five acres of land that Lloyd had given to them.

After graduating in June 1958 from Watershed High School, Wilma left Sienna to attend nursing school in the larger city of Tallahassee, located about forty-five miles east of Sienna. Alma had been extremely nervous about her youngest child leaving to live in a larger city, but Wilma would not be dissuaded, and her father reluctantly gave in to her moving to the big city to begin her studies as a nursing student. Malcolm made the decision to enlist in the United States Army and had left town by the time Wilma graduated from high school.

Unfortunately, one week before graduation in May 1962, Wilma received a call from her father to come home immediately because her mother, Alma, was ill. She had fallen on the floor while washing dishes in the Hamiltons' kitchen.

Martha Hamilton heard the thud and glass breaking on the floor, and when she ran to the kitchen, Alma's face was drooping on one side and her speech was slurred.

Martha yelled from the kitchen door for Lloyd to come and then used the phone in the kitchen to call the operator to send the ambulance. Upon entering the kitchen, Lloyd immediately called Sienna Memorial Hospital and spoke to the hospital president, Wayne Novack, telling him that they had called for the ambulance to pick up Alma, and he wanted her taken to Sienna Memorial's emergency room for treatment and admission to the hospital.

Wayne said, "Sure, Lloyd, no problem. I'll call the emergency room right now. I'll radio the ambulance attendants too. Glad to help."

Wayne knew he still owed Lloyd over five hundred dollars from when his oldest son had gotten into trouble with the law and needed bail money. Lloyd was the only person Wayne could think of to call who would not gossip either about the incident or about Wayne asking to borrow money. Lloyd had been patient with Wayne and was accepting the payback in small installments.

Lloyd responded, "Thanks, Wayne; I knew I could count on you."

Alma was admitted to Sienna Memorial without any resistance or verbal complaints.

By the time Wilma arrived at Sienna Memorial a few hours later, her mother was in a coma from a hypertensive stroke with bleeding on the brain. Entering the hospital room, Wilma saw her mother lying unresponsive on the bed, with her father sitting in the chair at the bedside holding his dear wife's hand.

Wilma hugged her father, held her mother's other hand, and quietly called her name. Alma opened her eyes, gave an ever-so-slight nod of her head, took a deep long breath ... and died. Wilma's heart ached as she placed her head on her mother's chest and cried. She knew then that she would return to Sienna to be with her father.

The town of Sienna was different from most in the South as it was not really segregated, and this was because over 80 percent of the population was Black. It had been that way since the 1850s, most likely due to the large tobacco farming industry and the need for field labor, even after slavery was abolished. Sienna Memorial

Hospital was considered integrated because the hospital would accept some Black patients under special circumstances, but the smaller Carver Hospital served predominately Black patients. Wilma's first job was at Carver Hospital, and she had recently moved over to Sienna Memorial to work as a registered nurse for the intensive care unit (ICU).

In her last year of college, Wilma met Larry Hinson, who was majoring in business administration, and his main goal was to have his own auto mechanic business. Wilma thought this was very ironic, because you didn't need a business degree to work on cars. However, Larry believed he could start the business and grow the name and reputation to where he could reproduce the business in multiple towns. Wilma thought Larry was kind of weird, but in a good way, so she gave him enough of her time, until one day she realized that she had fallen in love with him. After her mother died, Larry attended the funeral and returned a week later to ask Wilma's father for permission to marry Lloyd's only daughter.

Three months later, Wilma and Larry were married at Hillside Baptist Church. Larry moved to Sienna and started an auto mechanic shop, and within three years the business had grown to the point that he opened a second shop on the western outskirts of Tallahassee.

As Larry drove down Hampton Street to pick up the children from school, he wondered if Wilma was feeling any better. Their oldest child, Christopher, was five years old and was in the first grade at Troutville Elementary, while their two-year-old twin daughters, Carmen and Crystal, attended the day school at Hillside Baptist. Both places were within three blocks of each other, so it didn't take Larry long to pick them up, and the trip home seemed quick as Christopher talked, seemingly nonstop.

Wilma awakened when she heard the sound of Larry's Ford truck pull into the driveway. She couldn't get up quickly enough to meet the children in the living room. The three ran into the bedroom, jumped on the bed, gave her hugs and kisses, and Christopher started describing in detail his day at school. Wilma smiled. It was good to have the kids and Larry home.

* * *

It was 6:58 p.m. when Doc arrived at the emergency room to be on duty. He and the other two doctors in town would rotate covering the ER. A week had passed since the assassination of Dr. Martin Luther King Jr., and the town was still on edge. He had seen the crowd gathering downtown and figured they would disperse as usual by 8:30 p.m. or so. He was wrong, and at 8:45 he could hear the sirens going and police horns blaring. The ambulance started bringing in the wounded patients. Doc had to call in both Dr. Smith and Dr. Laney to assist. They spent the rest of the night in the ER, suturing up lacerations of all types. He would learn what happened in bits and pieces from the officers, because it seemed each patient had a different version of how they were injured and what incited the riot. Doc found out later that Willie Collins, a Black local cobbler, had closed up his store and was headed downtown.

The story as accounted by Willie was that in his hand was a shoe hammer that he needed to replace, and he was going to stop by the hardware store the next morning. As he was walking up Adams Street, approaching the larger crowd of Black peaceful protestors, he heard someone call out, "Hey, turn around slowly, and drop your weapon." Willie said he was confused and not sure what to do, so he ran. He heard a shot, and pain ripped through his leg. He thought the voice might have been police officer Isaac Henderson, but he couldn't say for sure. At that point, the rioting started. Two fellow Black men helped Willie into their car and drove him to the ER. With the windows down, they could hear the sound of windows breaking downtown, and smoke was beginning to rise in the air.

It was confirmed later the next day that the Black policeman, Isaac Henderson, had fired the shot that injured Willie.

As history unfolded in major cities across America, that was the one and only riot in Sienna during the 1968 unrest, and it was initiated by Willie's flesh wound from a Black police officer's gun.

CHAPTER 2

"Blessed are the pure in heart: for they shall see God."
(Matthew 5:8 KJV)

Doc had to close the office after the riot that occurred on Thursday, April 11, but by the following Monday, April 15, the office was back open. Tensions were still running high, and it was taking some extra attention and effort to gain credibility with the older Black parents and grandparents of the children who would come to his office and show up for care in the ER. It was well worth the extra time, and Doc believed it was the right thing to do as a Christian. They had every right to be hesitant and maybe even suspicious.

Months had passed. It was now November, and Alice had given birth to their fourth son on October 2. Doc was sleep deprived and longing for a good night's sleep. It was a blessing to have Nathaniel born healthy and without any birth defects, and while Doc certainly was thankful, he was also tired.

After completing his hospital rounds at Sienna Memorial, Doc arrived at the office just before 8:00 a.m., giving him about thirty minutes before Betsy would arrive. Letting himself in the back door, he went straight to his office and opened the window blinds. With his office situated on the corner, he had a good view of Main Street, and he had developed the habit of looking out the window as he daydreamed or contemplated what to do about patient diagnostic dilemmas. The fall season had ushered in beautiful autumn colors, and he prayed that his siblings were doing well—four sisters and one brother. He was the second oldest of his parents' six children and by far the most quiet and understated. He had quickly become known as the best doctor in town.

Walking up the sidewalk in the direction of the high school was Ronnie Ellis. Doc put his right index finger on his face as he thought about Ronnie. There was something about the seventeen-year-old that made him different from most of the kids his age. He was quiet and avoided eye contact in the most extreme way. His family owned Ellis Funeral Home and Mortuary, the major provider of burial services for Blacks and other minorities in Sienna (although there were very few Mexicans and Native Americans compared to Blacks). Doc had seen Ronnie in the office the week before for a rash that was easily diagnosed by Doc as *tinea versicolor* (a fungal infection), and Doc had given him a prescription for 2 percent selenium sulfide cream as treatment. It had been difficult to obtain a medical history from Ronnie, and Ronnie's aunt, Carrie Bartley, had answered even basic questions on his behalf.

Occasionally, Alice would substitute at the local high school, and she had mentioned to Doc the introverted personality of Ronnie. He was an A student who kept to himself because he was teased by the other students for being an undertaker's son. He wondered if Ronnie could see him standing at the window, but then decided Ronnie probably couldn't see beyond the blinds.

Ronnie was enjoying the walk to school when he felt someone looking at him. He looked to his left and thought he saw the flicker of the blinds from the window of Dr. Hamilton's office. It was too early for the office to be open, but then he saw the doctor's car in the back of the building. Maybe the doctor was watching people from his office window? Ronnie picked up his pace. He didn't like being spied on, and he would try to remember that Doc might have a tendency to watch the happenings of the town from his window. "Doc is strange," Ronnie whispered to himself. The business of taking care of dead people made him keenly aware of the living.

His father often said, "It's not the dead you have to worry about, it's the living! They are always up to no good, but the dead—well, they have done all their wicked deeds, and now they are saints."

Given the way the kids treated him at school, Ronnie agreed wholeheartedly with his father. It wouldn't be long before he would graduate and head off to college, and he wished he could speed up the time. He had already decided to attend the junior college in north Florida that offered the Associate of Science degree in Funeral Services, and then he would return home to help manage the family business. He whistled his favorite song as he got closer to the school—the "Battle Hymn of the Republic."

Once Ronnie was out of view, Doc walked over to his desk to look over the morning schedule. A few minutes later, the phone rang, and it was Alex Hamilton, Doc's brother. Alex spoke before Doc could say hello.

"Hello, Steve. How's it going for you this morning? I saw you drive by the office a few minutes ago. I am up earlier than usual, just trying to get as much fertilizer out as I can before Thanksgiving. Trying to help Daddy with the farming and all."

Doc responded, "Yeah, Alex, I'm glad you are here in town. That agricultural degree you got from Florida is paying off for Daddy. He said the crops are doing really well the last two years or so. Anyway, I didn't sleep well last night. You know how it is; Nathaniel is not sleeping but a few hours at a time during the night." Doc's voice trailed off.

Alex continued, "I was calling about the parade. I think the town's settled down fairly nicely now from the earlier unrest, so it might be good for us to go ahead with it. What have you heard from the sheriff about the racial stuff?"

Doc really didn't understand Alex's concern, and he hadn't talked to Sheriff Skifton, so he decided to say, "No, I don't think there will be any problems, and I had heard that the council decided to proceed with the parade. You know the church and Daddy spend a lot of time getting the parade just so."

There was a pause, and then Alex said, "I tell you, ... we don't have that much time now to pull it off. Still, though, I think we can make it happen. You know how Daddy likes to have that parade go through town and by the church and your office. He acts like he's the daddy of the town, despite all the new folks here in the last ten years or so."

Doc chuckled and replied, "Yep, he sure does, but he's fairly modest about it. Only the family knows how he really feels about it."

"I guess you're right. I'll keep you updated," Alex said as he hung up the phone.

Doc held the receiver for a few seconds before he hung it in the cradle. Alex sounded too jovial for the time of day, especially since he wasn't a morning person. When they were growing up, Alex would sleep for as long as their parents would allow—which usually wasn't very long at all. The cheerfulness of Alex was probably related to his excitement about the parade. Doc's father wasn't the only one in the family who loved the town's parade—Alex was a very close second. Alex's wife, Sue, was also from Sienna, and similarly to Doc and Alice, both were members of the First Presbyterian Church. Their son, Alexander Lloyd Hamilton II, and their daughter, Melissa, were growing up in a similar way to Alex and his siblings, in which church, school, and family were the central components of their lives. The trappings and distractions of big city living were not concerns for those choosing to live in Sienna.

As for the farm, shade tobacco was still the major crop, but Lloyd was also farming tomatoes and mushrooms. He still had enough loyal workers to maintain the acres for farming, as it didn't seem that anyone else in the family would become farmers. It was just as well, since Lloyd and Martha had done it out of necessity and not out of love for the agricultural process. Some of the land was now used for hunting, and the Hamilton family could often lease it out to the hunting club for a significant amount of money.

The day in Doc's office got off to a busy start, and Betsy couldn't keep up with the phone calls and the patients who were coming in. By noon, Doc knew they would be there until nightfall.

Four hours later, Doc went into the exam room to see Sheriff Carl Skifton. Sure, he was a pediatrician, but he would see adults if they came into the office for acute problems. Fortunately, Doc had served as a medical officer in the Army while he was stationed in Germany, and it had given him experience seeing adults in the emergency room.

Sheriff Skifton exclaimed, "Man, Doc, I sure am glad you could see me. I don't know what the hell is wrong with me. My belly is sure hurting bad."

"When did the pain start?" Doc asked.

"Well, I've had trouble with it hurting up at the top and in the middle, off and on, for about three months. I tried laying off of spicy foods and what have you, but last night, it got the best of me. I've been hurtin' and throwin' up ever since."

Doc patted the exam table while saying, "Lay down on the table here and let me examine your abdomen."

Despite all the viral gastroenteritis that Doc had seen over the last week, he almost knew, even before he examined Sheriff Skifton, that this diagnosis would be different. Doc's intuition as a physician was excellent.

Sheriff Skifton was groaning as he positioned himself supine on the examination table. Every movement seemed to cause him discomfort. Doc noted the extreme distress that the Sheriff was in and proceeded to palpate his abdomen, revealing tenderness in the upper right quadrant with guarding and rebounding.

"Sheriff, we'll have to admit you quickly to the hospital. You have an infected gallbladder. Did your wife drive you over?"

"Yes, Doc, she did. She's there in the waiting room."

Doc opened the door and called out for Betsy. When she entered the room, he told her that the diagnosis was acute cholecystitis and quickly gave her the orders for Sheriff Skifton. He asked that she get Dr. Laney on the phone, because he would be the one to perform the surgery. In the Army, Doc learned and assisted with some of the more common adult surgical procedures, which came in handy in the small town of Sienna, when the only general surgeon needed a first assistant.

Within two hours, Doc was scrubbing in to go into the operating room with Dr. Laney to remove the Sheriff's gallbladder. Fortunately, there was no perforation of the gallbladder, and the cholecystectomy was done without any complications. There were ten stones in the gallbladder as well as evidence of chronic and acute inflammation. It was well after 10:30 p.m. before Doc arrived home. Alice had fallen asleep on the couch. He gently awakened her, and they talked about the events of the day—it had been a long and tiring one. They talked about Wilma joining the office as the second nurse and about hiring a receptionist for the front office. The workload was becoming too much for Betsy to handle alone.

Two days before Thanksgiving, Wilma stopped by the office in the evening to see Doc. Betsy had left, but Doc was still there. He had asked her several weeks before to come by, but she had been so busy working her shifts at the hospital and then trying to hurry home to take care of the kids and Larry that there seemed to be little time for any extra socializing. Wilma felt guilty about taking so long to get by to see Doc. The Hamilton family had been kind to her parents, and to Malcolm and herself.

Wilma smiled and said, "Hello, Doc."

"Wilma, come now, you can call me Steve," he said as he shook her hand and led her into his office.

"I'm sorry it took me so long to stop by. First, I got sick with the stomach virus that was going around, and then after that I was running from work to home and . . ."

Doc interrupted, "Wilma, it's okay. You don't need to apologize. We're all busy these days trying to take care of the sick. Listen, we have gotten really busy at the office, and Betsy really needs some help. We are seeing more Black patients in the office now, and I thought it would be good, well, if you were willing, to join us here at the office."

"Steve, do you mean you want me to come here and work as a nurse?" Wilma was surprised at the request.

"Yes. You seem shocked."

"Well, I am. I don't know that the town has progressed enough for me to join your office. What do you think your White parents with their kids will think about that?"

"I think it will be fine. You are a well-respected nurse at the hospital, so why would it be any different here at the office?"

Wilma smiled and said, "Steve, I really appreciate you thinking of me and offering me the position. Let me think about it. I would like to talk to Larry about it. I do enjoy taking care of the really sick patients at the hospital, so this would be quite a change for me, since the clinic patients are not as ill as the ICU patients whom I take care of at Sienna Memorial."

Doc nodded affirmatively. "I understand. Sure, think about it and get back to me as soon as you can. We really need the help."

"Okay, I will," Wilma responded as she opened the door to leave.

Later that night, after Wilma had gotten the kids to bed, she and Larry discussed the job offer from Doc.

"Larry, I finally had the chance to stop by the office to see Steve."

"What happened?" Larry asked.

"Well, he asked me to come and work for him. He said the office has gotten too busy for just him and Betsy to handle."

"Well, what do you think?" Larry was very interested in hearing Wilma's response.

"Baby, I don't think the time is right. I'd hate for him to lose White patients because he hired a Black nurse. Maybe I'm being overly sensitive. I mean, you have White customers."

"I do have White customers, but that's partly because they tried some of the White mechanics and had to spend more money and their cars still didn't run right. I don't know if medicine and auto mechanics are on the same level for a good comparison. Me touching a person's car is not the same as you touching them as a nurse. You know what I mean, baby?"

THE HEART ALWAYS KNOWS · 17

"Yeah, I do. I don't want to turn Steve down, but I think this might not be the best thing for me to do right now. I like having the shift work and being off during some of the weekdays, although working weekends and holidays during the year is not great."

"That's a thought. It would be good to have my sweetie home on every holiday," Larry said.

Wilma said softly, almost as if speaking to herself, "I'll pray about it some more. It sounds like you are fine with whatever I decide?"

"Yes, either way is fine with me." Larry assured Wilma.

That night, Wilma spent a great deal of time talking to God. When she awakened the next morning, Wilma knew that she had the right answer to give to Doc, and she was glad that it had not taken her long to reach a decision.

The next day, Wilma stopped by Doc's office again and told him that she really appreciated him thinking of her for the position, but she decided it was not the right time for her to make the move away from the hospital. He nodded and said he understood. As Wilma left the office, Doc felt a sadness that he couldn't quite explain. He looked out of his office window and watched Wilma drive down the street and turn the corner. Maybe he could find a second nurse before Christmas. The town was gearing up for the Thanksgiving parade tomorrow, and he would drive out to his father's house for the traditional Thanksgiving family dinner.

With Martha's help, Alice delivered the last Thanksgiving Day baskets to the deacons at the Hillside Baptist Church. She only had five churches on her list. Each year, the Sienna Women's Club would ask the various churches to submit names of families whom they felt qualified for a Thanksgiving basket. The list of needy families would go through an evaluation by the Sienna Women's Club, although the evaluation only consisted of where the family lived and what type of job the parents had. As the town had grown, the list had slowly grown as well, but it was still under seventy baskets. After leaving Hillside, she headed to the country club to meet Doc for dinner. Her mother, Ellen, was watching the boys, and it would give her and Doc a chance to have some time together.

There were few people dining in the country club when Alice arrived. Doc was talking outside with the club owner, Edgar, but he quickly made his way over to the car and opened the door for Alice. They hugged and made their way into the club's dining area.

Fortunately, the smokers were in the back of the club, allowing Doc and Alice, who were definitely not smokers, the opportunity to have a pleasant meal in the front part of the club's dining room. After a prime rib dinner and dessert, the couple traveled in separate cars back to their home. Doc sat down on the sofa while Alice sat in the recliner with her knitting yarn. Frank Sinatra was singing softly from the radio on the kitchen table.

"Well, Alice, baby, Wilma gave me her answer. She's not going to come to the office to work," Doc said in a quiet voice.

"I'm not really surprised, Steve, although I know you are probably disappointed. Honey, I'll come and help you until you can find a couple of people to help out. My mom and your mom can help watch the kids for us. I really don't mind."

"I know you don't, and I really appreciate it. I think Samantha who works in the emergency room might be interested. I'll ask her."

"Yes, she's nice and will probably get along well with Betsy. Though, I only know her from the Sunday school class."

Much later, as Doc lie in the bed looking up at the ceiling, he couldn't fall asleep. He had been back in town for just over a year, but already his practice was busy enough that he was having staffing issues. He was tired and just wanted to rest tomorrow, but instead he would get up early, make rounds at the hospital, go to the Thanksgiving Day parade, and then drive the fifteen miles out to the homestead where his parents lived. He had a feeling of dread that he just couldn't shake off.

The phone was ringing by the bed, and Alice reached over Doc to answer it. It was just after 4:00 a.m.

"Alice, this is Deputy Peters. Sheriff Skifton is still recovering from his surgery. Sorry to bother you, but can you hand the phone to Doc? I've got some really bad news."

"Sure, Deputy. Hold on." Alice reached over to shake Doc.

"Steve, wake up. Wake up! It's Deputy Peters on the phone."

"Hey, Deputy, what's going on?" Doc was still groggy as he took the phone receiver from Alice.

"Well, Doc, it seems that Wilma and Larry and the kids started out of town in the early morning, headed to visit his parents for the holiday. Seems he lost control of the station wagon. You know, there are so many blind spots on that curvy part of the highway. Seems he hit a deer, lost control, and went over the embankment. The car burst into flames."

"Oh no, Peters. . . . Please tell me a miracle happened . . . ?"

"No, Doc, I'm sorry. They were all killed. By the time we got out to the scene, it was too late. Those poor kids, all dead. We ain't even sure we can identify the bodies. I'm just so sorry, Doc."

Doc's voice cracked as he said, "Thanks, Peters, for calling me. I guess there's not much for me to do, and I'll let Alice know."

Alice had heard the conversation because Deputy Peters always talked louder than most. She got up and walked over to the side of the bed where Doc was and held him tightly. There were no words to express their sadness and disbelief. He got up, dressed, and headed out to the scene of the crash.

By the time he arrived, the area had been roped off, and the law enforcement and forensics teams were in full force. There wasn't a whole lot to consider, really. The deer was dead, the car was down over the embankment, and personal items from the suitcases were scattered across the ground. The scene was quite overwhelming to look at.

Doc reflected on the last twenty-four hours. He had had a feeling that something bad was going to happen. Some would call it a premonition. When he left for college, he had planned to go into the ministry, because he felt he was called to minister to others.

But after the first semester, he believed the calling was to pursue medicine and help others in that way. His relationship with the Lord continued to develop, and even as a young child he was sensitive to things of the heart. He had tried to intercede in prayer throughout the day for all who came to his mind, hoping to relieve the inner feeling he had that there was something very negative in the works. If only he had prayed specifically for Wilma and her family, maybe they would still be alive. He knew in his heart that was not the case. For whatever reason, the Lord allowed this to happen, as unfair as it seemed. Doc whispered to himself, "The Lord is all-knowing and omnipresent, and I have to accept that as the truth. Help me, Lord."

The tragic death of Wilma and her family rocked the small town of Sienna. There was not enough time to cancel the Thanksgiving parade, and so it proceeded based on tradition. Doc rode on the lead float, along with his parents, Alice, and the boys. Lloyd and Martha were always the main sponsors of the parade, with the financial assistance of the Sienna Bank, First Presbyterian Church, and the city council. They had just enough time to have a sign placed on the float that read *In Memory of Larry, Wilma, Christopher, Crystal, and Carmen Hinson*. There were forced smiles, waving of hands, and wiping of tears as the float made its way down the road. It was so hard to have even a small sense of joy and thanks.

On Thanksgiving evening, Doc knocked on the door, and he could hear the footsteps approaching from inside the house. Henry Washington was a large, burly man with hazel-green eyes and smooth dark skin. He opened the solid door and then the screen door and reached out to shake Doc's hand. Doc accepted the handshake and held on for a few seconds.

As the two walked into the living room, Doc said, "Mr. Henry, I am so sorry for . . ."

"I know, Doc; you don't have to say no more. I know you loved Wilma like a sister, and she loved you like a brother."

Henry's voice trailed off as he said, "I just can't believe she and those kids are gone. Just like that. Just like a thief in the night, the

Lord done took them away from me. And that Larry, why that Larry, he was a real smart man and a darn good mechanic. I loved him. I loved all of 'em. Now I got nobody but Malcolm, and I don't know when he can get away. I don't even know if he can make it home for the funeral. He's in Germany, you know, and that's just so far away, and what if they don't let him out, you know, let him out to travel from Germany to come to Sienna."

Doc was a good listener, so that's what he did. He sat quietly and let Henry talk for as long as he wanted. They each drank a Coca-Cola, and Doc asked Henry to call him with anything he thought he might need. There were already plans to have the funeral for all five family members at Hillside Baptist Church, and the burial would be there as well. Of course, there was not much left to bury, since the bodies were burned badly from the crash, but recognition was made of the few things that were thrown from the car. Nothing survived the fire, and the investigators described the fire as a crematory for the bodies due to the intense heat. After an hour, Doc left and drove back into town.

Nine days later, the funeral was held for the Hinson family. Larry's family traveled from North Carolina for the service, and they made the decision to bury him with his wife and children in Sienna. Malcolm sat in the church next to his father and served as one of the pallbearers. He was a younger version of his father: tall, muscular, and a little more quiet than Henry. At the graveside, Doc had a chance to talk to him.

"Hello, Malcolm; it's good to see you. I'm sorry it had to be on such a sad occasion." Doc reached out and shook Malcolm's hand.

"It's good to see you too, Steve. I wanted to come home sooner, but I just never seemed to have enough time to make the trip. I sure wish I had found a way to do it." Malcolm wiped the tears that flowed down his cheek with a white handkerchief.

He was dressed in his Army uniform with the Sergeant emblem designation. Several young men from Sienna had already died in the

Vietnam War, and the draft was still in place. Doc was thankful to have Malcolm back in Sienna, even if only for a brief period.

"Steve, I think I'll plan to stay in the Army and make a career of it. Well, I'll at least stay in for twenty years. I think I can continue to advance, and well, you know, Wilma always wanted me to go to college, so I think I'll do that too, thanks to the G.I. bill. It would be good to do it in honor of her. Wilma was such a loving sister. We wrote to each other at least once a month, and she so liked being a nurse."

Doc nodded his head, "Yes, she did enjoy taking care of patients and being a nurse. She was good at it too. The whole town will miss her. I'll keep an eye on your father, and you stay safe and come back when you can."

"I will, Steve. I won't stay away so long. You just never know..."

CHAPTER 3

"Who is the greatest in the kingdom of heaven? And Jesus called a little child unto him, and set him in the midst of them."
(Matthew 18:1–2 KJV)

Doc arrived back to Sienna shortly after dark. It was session time for the Florida Legislature; it was now 1970, and this was his obligatory trip to Tallahassee.

This trip, however, was different, and was done to thank the legislators for their support and to reaffirm the commitment to providing care to the rural and underserved population of Sienna.

Doc, along with three Tallahassee physicians and several physicians affiliated with the University of Florida, had spoken at each session at the Capitol for the four previous years in hopes of getting Medicaid implemented for the low-income citizens of Florida. Doc's last trip in 1969 had given them great hope that the Florida legislature would make sweeping changes and reforms to advance health care for citizens in the state. It had been a long, hard battle with the legislators, but finally the advocacy role of the physicians, hospitals, and community supporters prevailed, and the state of Florida had approved Medicaid coverage for low-income and disabled citizens. Even though Florida was one of the last states to implement the program, it was finally done!

Nationally, Medicare and Medicaid were enacted in 1965 as Title XVIII and Title XIX of the Social Security Act, because it was known that seniors were the population most likely to be living in poverty.[2] However, Doc's experience had proven otherwise. There were many teenage and adult women who were pregnant and suffering from poor nutrition and inadequate perinatal care, and the birth deliveries of the working poor or unemployed were done by midwives. Doc knew the midwives very well, and most were excellent at delivering the noncomplicated births, but after delivery babies would show up to his office malnourished and requiring extensive care. As a pediatrician, there were other resources that he had to use and know about. The Children's Bureau program was in place and was now known as Children's Medical Services, with a Florida medical director and many pediatric residents who gave their time to support the care needed for the children. The social workers and public health workers were necessary contacts and relationships to have and cultivate.

One of the benefits to children on Medicaid was the Early and Periodic Screening, Diagnosis, and Treatment (EPSDT) comprehensive health services that had been established in 1967 for all children receiving Medicaid. This benefit would now be available for the children in Sienna.

Finally, the many years of advocacy had paid off, and Doc smiled with satisfaction. He was back at his home, where his loving wife and children lived with him. Doc readied himself for bed; he laid down after a long but good day. As he felt the soft pillow under his head, he quickly drifted off to sleep.

Other victories would follow for Doc and his fellow children's advocates; in 1972, a supplemental food program was started in a few states. Then in 1974, the first site opened in Kentucky, under the Women, Infants, and Children (WIC) program. As a federally funded program, WIC supplied, at no cost, healthy foods, nutrition education and counseling, breastfeeding support, and referrals for health care and community services.[3]

In 1974, the WIC program came to Sienna, and then in 1975 it was established as a permanent program by legislation. The support that this provided to many in the community was definitely needed, and the number of malnourished children that Doc was seeing in the practice started to decrease.

Government support wasn't the only thing that was growing. Doc's pediatric practice was bursting at the seams. He had already added another receptionist and nurse, but more help was needed. He was seeing over seventy patients a day, and Alice was concerned that he was wearing himself thin. He was trying to carve out time for their four boys, Bible study at church, children community benefit activities, and the list went on and on. If he wanted to take any time off for a vacation, he would have to line up the general practitioners to cover his practice while he was away. That sometimes proved more difficult than Doc could ever have realized prior to opening his solo practice.

It was a typical spring day when Mr. Curtis Wray walked into the office with his six-year-old son who had a rash. While Doc was examining the little boy, Curtis said, "Hey, Doc, your office is crazy busy! There's no room to sit in the waiting area, and you know, the wait is, like, hours to get the boy in to see ya."

Doc replied, "Yeah, I know Curtis, I'm sorry. I'm going as fast as I can, but I want to give good care too, so it takes a little time."

"Oh, no, Doc, I'm not criticizing. I was just thinkin' that I know this lady doctor up at the Chattahoochee hospital. You know, I teach math classes up there to the psychiatric patients. Well, anyway, she's a real good doc, I think, and if I remember right, she's in pediatrics and psychiatry, and her name is Dr. Maria Campos. If you have any interest, I could see if you two could talk. It might give you some needed help here in the office."

"Curtis, that would work for me. Every time I think I have someone to join me in the practice, something goes wrong. It's just hard to recruit other doctors to come to live in a small town."

Curtis smiled and said, "Well, I'll talk to her and let you know."

Doc replied, "Thanks, Curtis. Thanks so much. Now for little Curtis Jr. here—he looks as if he has chicken pox. I'll notify the school. Take him home, and on your way, stop by the drugstore. Betsy will call them about what you'll need to use for the itching. Keep everybody away from him who hasn't had chicken pox yet. He should be fine in a couple of weeks, but give us a call if you notice any high fevers or bad coughing."

"Thanks, Doc, I will."

One month later, Dr. Maria Campos and Doc met in Sienna at the local diner. It was a good meeting. After leaving the diner, Doc showed Dr. Campos the office, and they agreed that she would start in June for three days a week while she transitioned the practice in Chattahoochee to a different physician.

Flyers were made to introduce Dr. Campos to the town, parents, and local leaders.

The cases of chicken pox were increasing in the community. Doc had just finished seeing Carrie Ellis Bartley's daughter, Sabrina, who was now six years old and doing well in school. Sabrina had the classical vesicular lesions of the chicken pox virus. She noticed the first few fluid-filled blisters a few days prior, and like most parents, Carrie thought it was from poison ivy. But over three days it had rapidly spread to other parts of her body. Sabrina had a low-grade fever of 100.4, so Doc recommended Tylenol, calamine lotion, and low doses of Benadryl, but only if the itching became too unbearable. He advised Carrie to keep her at home and give the office a call if the fever was not controlled with the Tylenol or if she had any concerns at all.

The office remained busy for the rest of the day, and it was good to have Dr. Campos as part of the practice to see patients and make hospital rounds. Most of the children admitted to the hospital only stayed a few days, which kept the census of inpatients very low.

Alice was happy that Doc had some help, and for the first time in four years, the family finally took a vacation. It was a week at Santa Rosa beach, which was only about a three-hour drive away, but it was wonderful to spend time reading, resting, and swimming in the Gulf of Mexico with the boys. They were growing up quickly, and Nathaniel, the youngest, was already six years old!

Doc returned the next week from vacation and met Dr. Campos for an early breakfast to catch up on things.

Dr. Campos started first. "Steve, the office was very busy, and there weren't too many emergency room visits, but I do have a concern, and we should probably see this kid back in the office today. Sabrina's mom called, and she's still running a fever from the chicken pox and not eating very well. Maybe she's got something else going on."

Doc furrowed his brow. "Maria, let's follow that up quickly. I'll call Sabrina's mom and have her bring Sabrina to the office or ER right away."

They both ate quickly, and Doc decided he would just stop by Carrie's house to see Sabrina since it was only two blocks away and on the route to the office.

When he arrived at Carrie's house, it was just after 7:00 a.m. He knocked on the door a few times, and Carrie finally came to the door.

"Who is it?" Carrie asked through the door.

"Carrie, it's Doctor Hamilton. Can you open the door? I stopped by to see Sabrina. I got the report from Dr. Campos about her fever."

Carrie opened the door and shook Doc's hand, while saying, "Doc, I sure am glad to see you. She's real sleepy this morning. Hard to get her to say anything."

Doc walked into the small bedroom in the front of the house, and Sabrina was lying on the bed with parched lips, very dry mucous membranes, and skin that was beyond the normal warmth to the touch with an ever-so-slight hint of a fine macular rash.

Doc didn't want to alarm Carrie too much, so he said, "Carrie, let me help out here, because Sabrina is very dehydrated. I'll take her over to the ER right away and get some IV fluids started on her and some medications to bring this fever down. She may have another kind of infection going on now, other than chicken pox."

Carrie, with tears streaming down her face, mumbled, "Okay, Doc, whatever you say. I trust you and I'll be on in just a few . . ."

Doc called from Carrie's house phone to the ER to let them know he was coming and asked the ambulance to be ready to transport Sabrina to Tallahassee. He knew from experience that he could get her to the hospital to get fluids and treatment started faster than the ambulance based on their location.

Doc picked up Sabrina and placed her on the back seat of the car, and Carrie jumped in beside her daughter with Sabrina's head in her lap. Carrie had decided not to let Doc leave the house without her.

When Doc arrived at the ER, Sabrina's vital signs were critical. Her blood pressure was low but responded to IV fluids. A complete blood count (CBC), chemistry panel, and blood cultures were drawn. Before all the labs could return, the platelet count came back critically low, and the white blood cell count was high. The blood smear showed findings consistent with meningococcal infection. Sabrina was rushed by ambulance to Tallahassee Memorial Hospital with a diagnosis of sepsis and impending disseminated intravascular coagulation (DIC).

Despite all efforts made by the medical team, little Sabrina died a week later. Carrie was devasted. It was her second loss in just seven years; first her husband, and now Sabrina. When Doc received the phone call from the pediatrician in Tallahassee, he placed his head on the desk and sobbed.

Over the next several months, Doc struggled greatly with the loss of Sabrina. Had he and Dr. Campos delayed too long in getting Sabrina to Tallahassee? Were there any other warning signs that she had a secondary bacteremia? He had dreams about Sabrina and the trip to the ER that day. Her weak hand in his and her soft fading voice trying to talk to him. At each midweek service and every Sunday, he prayed for Carrie, Dr. Campos, and himself, that the Lord would grant them healing and peace. Doc made visiting Carrie a top priority on the first and third Wednesday mornings of each month. In some ways, Doc acknowledged to himself that Carrie was doing better than he was in coping with the passing of her daughter.

Carrie's dependency on Valium improved as Doc continued to visit with her. Just having a non-family member to talk with seemed to make all the difference. Doc introduced her to another parent who had lost a child around the age of Sabrina.

Hemmey Smith had lost his daughter, Hazel, to a ruptured brain aneurysm without any warning signs. His wife, Fiorna, had died just two years prior from a heroin overdose after leaving Hemmey and Hazel to move to Los Angeles in pursuit of an acting career. Hemmey never heard from Fiorna after that depressing day when he pleaded with her to not go and leave them, and Hemmey's first knowledge of Fiorna's whereabouts occurred when he received the call from the medical examiner, notifying him that Fiorna had been found on the floor in a motel bathroom with the needle still in her arm.

One year later, Doc and Alice drove back out to Hillside Baptist Church to attend the wedding of Carrie and Hemmey. Sheriff Skifton and Deputy Peters were in attendance, along with most of the sheriff's department staff. It was the first interracial marriage at Hillside and quite the talk of the town. Carrie was dressed in a beautiful cream-colored gown that made her smooth, dark-brown skin and long, pressed, black hair look even more stunning. Hemmey was dressed in his green deputy's uniform and looked as proud as any man could look with his auburn hair in a crew cut and his medium brown eyes beaming with satisfaction. Given the tragedies they had both suffered, it was wonderful to see them happy, and Doc was pleased to be a witness to the celebration.

CHAPTER 4

"And forgive us our debts, as we forgive our debtors."
(Matthew 6:12 KJV)

The years were rolling by quickly, and by 1977, Doc was in his tenth year of practice. The seasonal effect of tobacco farming was ending as the last tobacco crops were raised. Lloyd had already phased out tobacco years before as he saw it coming to an end. He was an independent farmer, but he had a packing house in town with a group of other farmers, and the major tobacco company also had a packing house. Given the integration that was present in the tobacco packing industry for Sienna, Lloyd made sure he had jobs for those who wanted to continue with farming. The mushroom and tomato crops were growing well, and there was plenty of work for those who wanted it. Sienna was fortunate in that way. They were starting to see more Mexicans come in and out of town as migrant workers, but they represented a minor part of the workforce, and the majority were still represented by the Whites and Blacks of Sienna who worked the farms.

One impact on Doc's practice was that the farmers sometimes would send a promise to pay for the child being seen, and this was accepted by Doc because, for the most part, the finances of the practice were doing well. Dr. Campos was still with him, as was Betsy. They had talked off and on about needing to get another doctor to help. They had already added another nurse, a receptionist, and two nurse assistants. The additional staffing helped to keep the flow going, and Dr. Campos and Doc routinely saw up to ninety patients a day.

The highlight for Doc each year were the school graduations. He would attend the graduations of the middle and high schools each year. Doc felt strongly that it was good to show the support for his pediatric patients who went on to become graduates of Sienna High School. There was a smaller high school too, Sienna West, but for the most part, Sienna High represented the largest number of graduates. Sienna High was known for graduating strong math and science students, and it was from this strength in the curriculum that Doc hoped he could encourage a handful of students each year to pursue chemistry or biology as a college major and then attend medical school. His hope was that in time, Sienna would have a strong community of practicing physicians, including pediatrics, family medicine, internal medicine, obstetrics and gynecology, and general surgery.

As the summer began, Doc started to seriously consider adding another physician to join the practice. It was time to expand out and offer more pediatric care to Sienna.

Dr. Arthur Watson was originally from Scotland, and his family had come over in the early 1940s and settled in New York as part of the mercantile trade. Dr. Watson was never really attracted to the Big Apple, and in his free time he loved being out in nature. He was an avid bird watcher and excellent photographer. Doc found out about Dr. Watson through one of the Tallahassee pediatricians, Dr. Matthew Soros. The two, Doc and Dr. Watson, met at the next American Academy of Pediatrics (AAP) meeting in 1978 in Atlanta. The two men were quite different in personalities; Dr. Watson was talkative and somewhat extroverted, which was strange, given the fact that he spent hours watching birds. Nonetheless, the two talked about Dr. Watson coming to visit the practice and spending a weekend in Sienna the first week in July. That would allow enough time for him to move his son and wife to Sienna if things ended on a positive note after the visit. Before the AAP meeting ended, Dr.

Watson decided he didn't need to visit. He liked Doc and would take him on his word.

In August, Dr. Watson, his wife, Nancy, and his son, John, moved to Sienna, and by the time school started, the practice was ready to branch out into accepting a larger number of new patients. Once again, introductory flyers were distributed, and the community was excited that a third pediatrician was coming to join Doc.

Although Medicaid had expanded a few years earlier, still over 60 percent of the infants were delivered by granny midwives. These midwives did a very good job, but the newborn infants needed to be seen at a weekly clinic. Doc found it somewhat unique and very pleasurable to increase participation in the Health Department's well-baby and well-child clinic. Additionally, he had formed very good relationships with the child protection team in Tallahassee, and so they recruited Doc and his two partners to be examiners for the state since they were already seeing some of the child abuse and neglect cases in their practice.

It was the one aspect of pediatrics that Doc wished was not a reality. Many of the abusers were family members or close friends of the families in which the children were victims. For Doc, Dr. Campos, and Dr. Watson, the goal was to detect potential signs of abuse as soon as possible in a child's life to prevent serious physical or psychological trauma. Many times, it worked, but unfortunately some children were victims before they could be seen in the office, and they would end up in the ER instead. Regardless, in their minds and hearts, as pediatricians, the three doctors were the advocates and protectors of the pediatric population.

Sallie O'Malley was only thirteen years old, and yet there she was in the office by herself for Doc to see her for some acute symptoms she was having. Betsy had already called Sallie's mother to confirm that it was okay for them to see her for what seemed to be cold symptoms.

Doc went into the room to see Sallie and asked Betsy to come in with him.

"Well, hello, Sallie, how are you doing? Sounds like you haven't been feeling very well. Tell me what's going on."

"Well, Doc, I just don't feel well. I feel tired and sad, and I can't eat, 'cause every time I do, it just comes right back up."

"Ms. Betsy will get your weight, and then we will run a few tests on you. We will be right back."

Once outside the door of the room, Doc whispered to Betsy, "Get a CBC, Chem panel, and HCG. Go back in there for me and find out when she had her last period and if she's been with any boys. You know, has she had any sexual intercourse? I'll go back in once we have more information. She will be more comfortable with you asking the first set of questions."

Betsy entered the room, and Sallie was sitting in the only chair in the room. Betsy sat on the rolling stool and held Sallie's hand.

"Now, Sallie, tell me, how is school going?"

"It's going okay, Ms. Betsy. I like my reading and English classes, and I've gotten better with math too." Her light blue eyes were very well complemented by the darker blue dress she had on, and her long blond hair was falling into her face as she avoided eye contact.

"Well, that's good, Sallie. Tell me now, do you have a boyfriend? Or are there any boys that you like being with?"

"I like Bobby, and he's been real nice to me. He's older than me, but he helps me with my school work and he's friend's with my brother . . ."

"Why, Sallie, don't cry. What's wrong?"

"Please don't tell my momma, Ms. Betsy, but I've been seeing Bobby and I'm scared, 'cause I know I've done wrong and I've been real bad by seeing him when Momma's not at home and my brother David is out working." She continued to cry.

"So, Sallie, you've been having sex with Bobby? Shh, shh, don't cry. We're gonna get some tests run on you, and then we'll have a sit down and talk again."

Betsy left the room, told Doc about the entire conversation, and Doc and Betsy went back into the room to examine Sallie.

As anticipated, her tests came back affirming that Sallie was pregnant, and given when she thought her last period was, she was already thirteen weeks along. The boy, Bobby, was sixteen, and once again Doc was facing another child having a child without any sense of the lifetime commitment it would require.

Betsy called Sallie's mother and asked her to come to the office, explaining that Doc wanted to talk to her. Diane O'Malley arrived about thirty minutes later, with her cashier's uniform still on from the Piggly Wiggly store where she worked.

Diane turned to Betsy and said, "Betsy, I hope it's not anything too bad going on with Sallie. I got here as soon as I could. What's wrong with her? You know, if she needs to stay out of school to get over this stomach bug, her older brother can watch over her. David's real protective of his little sister."

"Come on in, Diane, and have a seat in Doc's office. He'll be in shortly with Sallie."

Diane sat in one of the high-backed chairs in Doc's office, and a few minutes later, Doc entered, with Sallie just in front of him.

In a soft voice, Doc said, "Sallie, have a seat in the chair next to your mother, and let's talk about things, okay?" Sallie nodded while wiping away the tears that were streaming down her face.

Diane blurted out, "Well, what in the world is going on here, Doc? Sallie? Somebody tell me something!"

In a calm, soft voice, Doc responded, "Ms. O'Malley, thank you for coming in. Sallie doesn't have gastroenteritis. She is pregnant, and it seems the father is Bobby Cooper. I wanted to talk to you in person and not on the phone. She is probably about thirteen weeks pregnant."

Diane had a shocked look on her face and was speechless.

Doc continued talking. "We have a school now for teenage mothers, so Sallie can continue to go to school. She is really smart, and I would hate to see her drop out and not continue. We also have what is called the WIC program, and prenatal care is covered by Medicaid, so there is a lot of assistance available to her and to you.

Betsy will give you all the information. Do you want her to go to the health department or to the OB group here in town? There are also the midwives, but she is kind of young for them to deliver her. Just let us know, and we will get Sallie referred over to whichever office you choose."

Diane finally spoke. "I just can't believe this. Sallie, why didn't you talk to me? What am I going to do? You are so young, so young..."

Diane walked over and pulled Sallie up from the chair. Both were crying and hugging each other.

It was not what Doc had expected. But he should have known by now that parents could be unpredictable when faced with such harsh realities. In this case, he had expected Diane to be angry and lash out at Sallie. Diane's son, David, was eighteen and working part-time as a mechanic while attending the local junior college. Now, Doc could only hope that David would not perpetrate violence against Bobby. Sallie's father was away in the Navy and would not return from sea for another three months.

Diane interrupted Doc's thoughts by saying, "We will go and see the OB doc, Dr. Shipley. He delivered Sallie, and I think he will treat her well. I like him."

Doc walked them both out of his office over to the nursing area, where Betsy completed the necessary paperwork.

Later that night, around 8:30 p.m., police sirens were heard, and Doc was worried about the O'Malley's. Could it be that David had taken up matters against Bobby?

Doc rushed to get dressed and quickly called the Sheriff's office. Sallie, David, Bobby—they were all "his children," patients of the practice, and he couldn't just stay at home if they were in trouble.

"Hey, Doc, let me connect you to the Sheriff." The operator knew his number and his voice.

"Sheriff Skifton, this is Steve."

"Hey, Doc, yeah, there's trouble just west of town. I'm headed out now and will swing by your place to pick you up."

"Okay, thanks, Skifton."

A few minutes later, Sheriff Skifton picked up Doc, and they were on their way to the western outskirts of town. Over the radio, the deputies were calling in.

"Sheriff, are you almost here? You won't believe this, but it looks like George's boy was knifed down somehow. Stabbed in the stomach and neck, and his throat is sliced. Just a gruesome scene. You almost here? Whoever did this, ain't no way they can get all this blood off of themselves. Don't know if it was a carjacking gone bad or a robbery of some kind or what. Seems that Harry was trying to make it home. Either way, footprints seem to suggest there were multiple attackers."

"Good Lord! No! What the hell is going on in this county? Yeah, yeah, we're almost there. Doc's with me." Sheriff Skifton yelled, and he accelerated the vehicle.

Doc felt his heart sink. It wasn't Bobby or David, but George's son.

"Skifton, how can this happen in such a small town? It just makes no sense at all. Why, Harry was so happy the last time I saw him in the office. He had a job at Winn-Dixie and was making his own money. He wasn't willing to live off his father's money and stature of being the bank president," Doc asked, not expecting an answer.

"Beats me, Doc. Here we are. Lord a-mercy!" Sheriff Skifton gave an abrupt stop to the car, quickly opened the door, and made his way to the scene.

The crime scene had been roped off. Harry's body was being loaded in the ambulance by the two paramedics. They stopped when they saw Doc.

"Doc, you sure you want to see this?" One of the paramedics asked him.

"Yes, I do. He was one of my patients from the first year I opened my office."

They pulled the covering back, and there was Harry, bloody and lifeless.

He had put up quite a fight. His knuckles were bloody and bruised, and he had multiple large bruises on his upper arms. It seemed more than one sharp object was used to kill him. There was a large open wound in the abdomen, with part of the intestines showing. There was one large stab wound on the left side of the neck at the carotid artery, and then a large semicircular laceration going across his trachea. Indeed, it was a bloody, gruesome attack, and Doc had to step back and kneel down to keep from passing out. He was not prepared to see this tragedy. Harry was only eighteen and had just graduated from high school. He was planning to attend Davidson College, where Doc had graduated from, and then go to medical school at Emory. Harry had wanted to follow, as much as possible, the path that Doc had taken, and Doc had encouraged him to consider medical school at the University of Florida as an excellent option as well.

Now a young life was lost, and all the possibilities for Harry to pursue his dreams were gone. Doc couldn't believe it, even though Harry was lying lifeless before him.

Doc rode with the paramedics back to the hospital. He wanted to be at the hospital when George arrived to view the body in the morgue. When he arrived at the hospital, Doc went to the doctor's lounge to get a cup of coffee and then slowly made his way to the ER.

George was walking up to the desk. He spoke to the receptionist, "Hello, I got a call from Sheriff Skifton. He wanted me to come to the ER. Said something happened to Harry."

Doc reached the counter before the receptionist could respond. "Hey, George. Let's go into this other area where it's quiet so we can talk. Sheriff Skifton said I could talk with you."

As they walked down the hallway, George stopped suddenly and demanded, "Where's Harry? What in the hell is going on, Doc? Just tell me."

Doc turned and said, "George, I'm sorry, but Harry has died..."

"Wait, what? What are you saying, Doc? My boy is dead—that can't be—where... what... what happened?"

Sheriff Skifton arrived as George started to slump against the wall and onto the floor. He sat there on the floor with his head in his hands and sobbed.

Thirty minutes later, Doc, George, and Sheriff Skifton made their way to the morgue, and Sheriff Skifton only exposed Harry's face. The rest of the body would have been too much for George to see. By this time, George seemed to be in another world. Doc wasn't even sure if George heard anything that had been said to him by Sheriff Skifton. Harry was his youngest son and had been born when George was in his fifties, so it was often said by George that he hoped he could live to see Harry finish medical school. All of that hope was gone. No parent, regardless of their age when their child is born, expects to outlive their child. No one wants to bury their child.

As the weeks and then months went by, the investigation into the murder of Harry revealed that there were at least three attackers, and they were in a pickup truck with at least one side damaged when their vehicle stopped in the road to block Harry from passing. The Florida Department of Law Enforcement (FDLE) continued with the investigation. It would be six months before anyone was arrested.

In those six months, George continued to decline. His wife, Iona, seemed to handle her son's murder better than her husband, and she spent a lot of time at the First Presbyterian Church, volunteering. She went to noonday prayer every Wednesday and was leaning heavily on her faith. Iona prayed for whoever had killed her son, that the Lord would grant justice, for them to be found for their evildoings, and that the Lord would grant her the mercy and strength to forgive when the time came for justice.

George resented that the Lord had allowed this to happen. He stopped coming to church completely and resigned as President of First Sienna Bank. Since he was the founder of the bank and it was privately owned, the board of directors allowed him to name his oldest son, Jethro, as the next president.

Just before Christmas in 1978, four Black teenagers were arrested for the murder of Harry and later indicted. Details emerged that Harry was leaving from Winn-Dixie after being the last one to close up the cash register and put the money in the vault. The four were attempting to steal his Ford Mustang and take it for a joyride. Harry yelled at them, and they ran and jumped into a pickup truck that was already running. Harry and the four teenagers had gone to high school together; knowing which road Harry would take to get home, they sped away and waited for him on the most narrow part of the road. When they blocked the road and Harry stopped, they broke the window, and then the altercation happened, resulting in the brutal murder.

Doc was shocked and depressed over the senseless murder and now the destruction of four young men's lives. All of them had been patients in his practice, and it was a tremendous loss and tragedy for the community. He appeared in court for the sentencing and asked the judge to give them a chance for parole.

As the years passed by, he continued to pray for them—Allen, Rudy, Cleo, and Yancey. At the time of the murder, all were eighteen except Yancey; he was twenty, led the group with the idea, and gave the fatal stab to the carotid. He was convicted of first-degree murder and sentenced to life in prison without the chance of parole.

CHAPTER 5

"The Lord is nigh unto them that are of a broken heart; and saveth such as be of a contrite spirit."
(Psalm 34:18)

Fuswah County, which included Sienna, had grown to a population of roughly forty thousand by 1980. Doc was recalling the conversation that occurred while he was at home preparing to head over to the newborn nursery at the hospital.

Alice had started out by saying, "Hey, honey, do you remember that story I told you about my friend and college roommate Delores?"

"Which story, Alice? You know you have quite a few of them!" Doc chuckled about it.

Alice continued, "Well, she was the daughter of a physician, and in her senior year she was engaged to Billy, who was pre-med. Anyway, I woke up one night and she was crying, so I said, 'Delores, what's the matter?'"

"Well, what did she say? Why was she crying?" Doc asked.

"She said, 'Alice, I don't know if I can be married to a doctor.' Then I said to her, 'Well, Delores, you know you love Billy, so what's the problem?' She said to me that she knew she loved him, but that I just didn't understand. That she had seen her mother sit at the dinner table and talk and serve food, and her daddy wouldn't say a word. He was too tired to talk. She had seen it all. Well, she did marry Billy, and she enjoyed being married to him. But that was my first clue about silence at dinner."

"Alice, I'm sorry if I am so tired when I get home. Honestly, the boys are growing up so quickly. Tonight is graduation for Steven, and I don't even know where the years have gone. Over the last twelve years, we've been able to get away for some vacations at least once a year, and that's been good. I've learned every pay phone location in town and between here and Tallahassee. I guess it's no wonder that Steven isn't planning to go to medical school after his undergraduate. I guess I can't blame him for that. I appreciate all the time, energy, love, and dedication you've given to the boys."

"Steve, you've done the best you could, with such a large practice, and being part of the family medicine residency pediatric rotation program at Tallahassee Memorial for the last four years, where the young doctors come to the practice to rotate. It seems to make you happy, and you are not quite so tired as before."

Alice was known for having an outlook on life in which the glass was always half-full. No matter the circumstances, she could find a silver lining in a stormy sky.

Doc walked over and hugged Alice, saying, "I love you, Alice, and I will do whatever it takes to make you happy. Just tell me, okay?"

She nodded, but she knew there was no way she would ever intervene with his profession as a doctor. It was his calling, and she and the boys understood that—at least, she hoped the boys understood it.

Doc made it to the nursery, completed the rounds on the four newborns that were in the hospital, and then headed over to the office. There were no pediatric patients on the inpatient floor to check on, which shortened the hospital rounds. Doc felt fortunate to have the shorter time at the hospital; there would be a new resident rotating with them today, so he wanted to make sure he arrived early at the office to greet him. It was very rewarding being able to teach the residents; it made him feel energized to contribute to the training and education of the young physicians. It was his hope that maybe one of his sons would follow him into medicine, and he also had his eyes on a few of the incoming high school students who might have an interest in medicine. So far, he had not been able to mentor any high school students toward a medical career. Harry had been his last mentee.

Doc saw the clinic patients at a faster-than-normal pace because he wanted to make sure he was home in time to drive Alice and the boys to the graduation. Normally, Fridays were hectic in the clinic, and Dr. Campos and Dr. Watson had promised Doc that they would take care of any schedule overflows or emergencies. This was one occasion and celebration that he didn't want to be late for, or worse, completely miss. Betsy made sure he stayed on schedule because she wanted to attend the graduation too! Not only was "Stevie" (as she called him) graduating, but there were at least twenty other children from the clinic who were graduating as well. She was proud of all of them, and it wasn't easy to get kids from Sienna to stay with it and finish high school. So many of them dropped out of school to work on the farms. This evening was an occasion to celebrate, and she wanted to make sure that she and Doc were there to participate.

Doc arrived home in time to change into a dark-blue suit and tie. He helped Nathaniel, who was still learning how to tie the knot for a necktie, and he polished Nathaniel's shoes. Alice, Steven, Marcus, and Phillip were all ready by the time Doc finished helping Nathaniel get dressed.

It was nice to have the family in one car and headed to the first high school graduation of the boys.

Doc thought a lot about the graduates of the class of 1980, who were sitting there in the front of the gym about to receive their high school diploma. He was very proud of Steven, who graduated with a 3.95 GPA and was already accepted into Davidson College, where he planned to major in history and then attend law school. There were other teenagers from the practice who were graduating, and both Doc and Betsy were so proud of them. The parents clapped loudly and shouted out for their teenage graduate, and each time a child from the clinic graduated, Betsy and Doc would stand up and clap. It was an evening to celebrate. Earlier that day, Alice had cooked dinner at the house, and Betsy, her husband (Ron), Dr. Campos, Dr. Watson, the boys, the grandparents, and of course Doc, gathered at the home to eat dinner at the Hamiltons' house. Doc was glad that they had moved to a larger home a few years back, because the extra room was needed for the evening. Steven left to go out with his friends and was planning to spend the night at his best friend's Ezekiel's house. Overall, the day could not have turned out better, and it was a great way to enter into the weekend.

The next week, Iona stopped by the office after hours to see Doc. She wanted to talk to him about George. It had been two years since Harry's death, and George was not even close to a mental recovery. He spent most of the day in his room, in the dark, and would eat only minimal food. Iona went on to explain that he had lost so much weight that his clothes no longer fit. She was worried that he might commit suicide, so she had Jethro take all the guns away from the house. Doc felt great sympathy for Iona and offered to make a house visit to see George. He also thought it would be good to include Dr. Smith, the family medicine physician in town. Iona agreed that they could come visit tomorrow evening.

After Iona left, Doc sat at his desk and pondered what could have made those four boys take the life of Harry. It seemed so senseless. In the trial, it came out that at least two—Cleo and Yancey—were victims of child abuse. Their fathers would beat them for even minor misdoings and then lock them up in the closet or tie them to the bedpost for hours. In Yancey's case, it only led him to be more violent, and by the age of ten, he had been in and out of juvenile detention. Cleo was the first cousin of Yancey, and their fathers were brothers. There seemed to be a multigenerational line of mistreatment of the children in the family, and Cleo chose Yancey as his role model. Both wanted to join the Army, but Yancey's criminal record prevented him from being accepted as an enlistee.

Doc picked up the phone and called Dr. Smith's private line. Most likely, he was still at the office too.

"Hello, Dr. Smith, here."

"Hey, Lawrence, this is Steve. I've got a favor to ask of you."

"Sure, what's up? I owe you a few paybacks anyway," Dr. Smith said as he laughed.

"Well, you remember old man George, right?"

"Yeah, his boy was killed a few years back."

"Yep, that's right. Well, it seems he has signs of major depression, and his wife, Iona, you know, a real sweet lady, she came to see me just a while ago. Any chance you would be willing to take a ride out to their house late tomorrow, say around 6:00, to see him? She can't get him to come into town to see anyone. I would sure appreciate it if you could."

"Sure, Steve, that will work. I'll do it for you and for him. I saw him years ago as a patient in the office, but he wasn't much for seeing doctors. I'll come over to your office, and we'll ride out together in your car. I don't know how to wind my way back to their place."

"Okay, sounds good. Thanks, Lawrence."

The next evening, Doc and Dr. Smith met at the office and started the drive out to the Williamsons' place. They traveled west and as they turned off the main highway, about 500 feet later, they saw the cross marking the area where Harry died.

"Well, that's enough to make anyone depressed who drives by this spot every day," Dr. Smith mumbled.

Doc responded, "You're right. I forgot they had that placed at the scene. It's kind of hard to miss or ignore. I tell you, Lawrence, the image of Harry lying on that stretcher, lifeless, with his lips blue, was something I won't ever forget. I still have bad dreams about it."

"Yeah, I can understand that, Steve. Well, it's no wonder old man George is doing poorly. Let's see how good or bad it really is."

Doc turned right into the narrow paved private road leading up to the Williamson estate. It was a large red-brick colonial style house with two stories, and the front porch wrapped around both sides of the house. Sitting on at least five hundred acres, only about four acres were manicured. The rest of the land was wooded and used for hunting. The Williamsons had given up farming once George opened the First Sienna Bank back in the 1960s. Iona was sitting on the front porch in one of the white rocking chairs waiting for them. They got out of the car and greeted her, and then the three proceeded into the house.

The front windows had the draperies pulled back, letting in the sunlight that was coming from the westward setting sun. As they walked past the living room and the kitchen, down the hallway toward the master bedroom, the darkness seemed to overshadow them.

Iona knocked on the bedroom door and said, "George, the doctors are here."

She opened the door, and the three walked in. Doc was shocked at what he saw, and so was Dr. Smith. They both seemed frozen for a few seconds. George looked as if he had aged at least twenty years.

He was sitting in a chair with arms by the window, but the blinds were drawn, making the room fairly dark. A small lamp by the bed was on, but the light was dull. He was motionless, with no expression on his face, and the only sign of life was the slow lifting of his chest with each breath. His face was unshaven, and his long gray bread hung to his chest. He was looking into the distance at something that no one else could appreciate. He was thin, with temporal wasting and sunken eyes.

"Good evening, Mr. Williamson, we wanted to stop by and see you," Doc said.

Dr. Smith followed by walking toward him and taking his hand. "Tell me, what are you thinking about, George? What's on your mind?" A tear ran down one cheek and then another down the other cheek. That was the only response from George.

Iona spoke up, "That's all Jethro and I can get from him. Just tears. He will eat soup and drink liquids, but won't chew any solids. He is wasting away, and I don't know what to do."

Dr. Smith listened to George's heart and lungs. He palpated his stomach in the sitting position. With great effort, Dr. Smith and Doc were able to stand him up from the chair, but they couldn't get him to walk. So they gently lowered him back down into his sitting position.

The three left the room and went outside on the porch to talk. Iona brought out three glasses of sweet tea.

Dr. Smith started first. "Mrs. Williamson, have you thought about having your husband go somewhere to receive treatment and care? He has major depression and is in a catatonic state. I don't see him getting better here at home."

Doc chimed in, "I agree with that. What do you think? Is that something you would be willing to do? Is that something Jethro would consider?"

Iona replied, "Well, we've talked about it, but George always wanted to die at home. He never even liked to go to the doctor, as you both know. I would feel terrible if he died somewhere else. On the other hand, he's getting more and more feeble and needs more than what help I can provide."

They chatted for a while on the porch, rocking back and forth in the chairs while sipping the tea. Iona agreed to allow Dr. Campos to come out and visit George, given that she was a board-certified psychiatrist.

The next evening, Doc accompanied Dr. Campos to the Williamsons' house. The situation was the same, and after examining George, Dr. Campos talked to him.

"Mr. Williamson, you are suffering from a rare condition called major depression disorder with catatonia. Catatonia with bereavement has rarely been reported, and we need to get you to a place where others can help you. Mrs. Williamson, your wife, can't do it for you. There are medications and treatments that can help you. Otherwise, you will die here at home. Are you willing for us to do that for you?"

There was no acknowledgment from George.

As the three walked to the door, it was agreed that Iona would call the ambulance to take George to Sienna Memorial Hospital. Dr. Campos would admit him and then seek a transfer and admission to the Florida State Hospital in Chattahoochee, Florida, for treatment with antidepressants, antipsychotics, and maybe electroconvulsive therapy (ECT). Iona and Jethro would seek involuntary guardianship through the court system. Dr. Campos called the emergency room to make them aware that George would arrive by ambulance, Iona hugged them, and the two doctors left for the drive back to town. It would be a long road of recovery for George, but hopefully, he could get back to interacting with his loved ones instead of sitting at home and wasting away.

Jethro was a caring son toward his mother and father. George had done all he could to raise his sons in the fear and admonition of the Lord. Despite being a rich man, he had a meekness about him that made others like him.

Jethro continued the financial support of the annual Thanksgiving parade, and as Doc's parents were getting older, he and Alex agreed to take over their roles in the Thanksgiving parade. There was always a float in honor of Wilma and her family, with the name of the nursing scholarship on the side (Wilma W. Hinson Nursing Scholarship). Her family had raised enough money to fund a four-year scholarship for a resident of Fuswah county to attend Florida A&M University School of Nursing, Wilma Hinson's alma mater.

CHAPTER 6

"The father of the righteous shall greatly rejoice: and he that begetteth a wise child shall have joy of him."
(Proverbs 23:24)

The four years went by quickly to Doc, and he was now attending the graduation of his alma mater as Steven walked across the stage to shake the hands of the Davidson College's dean of academic affairs and the president of the college.

"Steven Hamilton Jr.—Summa Cum Laude." (*Clapping*)

So much had occurred between 1980 and 1984. Now Steven Jr. was a graduate of Davidson College and headed to Washington DC to work for Catholic Social Services to start a research project related to homelessness. He wanted to attend law school and was hoping that gaining some experience after graduation would help strengthen his application.

Doc's second-born son, Marcus, was attending North Carolina State University and majoring in mathematics, with the plan to obtain a master's degree.

Doc was certainly proud of all that his sons had and were accomplishing, and he understood that Alice was the glue holding it all together. She had been there for them all these years, attending the PTA meetings, going to the open houses, and participating as a Booster Club member for the basketball team and band. As much as Doc wanted to be at all the elementary, middle, and high school activities that his four sons participated in, the truth was that he probably only made it to less than a third of them. It wasn't that he didn't try to attend more, but there was always that one unplanned visit of a child to the emergency room or the one really sick kid in the office that would cause an obstacle for him to attend certain events. A sense of remorse came over Doc as he wondered if he could have done things differently. Maybe if he had planned his days out better, or even if he had gone to a larger city, with a large number of pediatricians in one group. The on-call schedule would have been better, and perhaps he would have made more money.

Sure, he and Alice had taken the boys on some nice vacations once he had support in the practice with Dr. Campos and Dr. Watson. The beach condo on Santa Rosa beach, for which he was able to save enough money and purchase back in 1978, was certainly nice. It had allowed them to get away to the beach for family time at least six times a year. Then there were the trips to several of the national parks, and even some missionary trips to Mexico, Guatemala, and Haiti. Despite all of that, Doc wished he could roll back the clock of time and spend more time with Alice and the boys.

The following month, in June, Doc received a very rewarding surprise.

Phillip, their third son, was graduating from Sienna High School as valedictorian, and he had a full scholarship to attend Rhodes College in Memphis, Tennessee, and major in psychology. On top of that, there were two patients whom Doc had mentored from middle school until now, and they were graduating as well.

The first student-patient was Aylen Hunt (*Aylen* is a Native American name, meaning "a clear individual; happiness"), the daughter of Haroldo (meaning "power, leader, ruler"), who was a Native American man of the Seminole tribe. Haroldo's family was known for choosing names that had special meanings for what they wanted their children to become. He was married to a Black lady, Marcelli, who died when Aylen was very young, and Haroldo never remarried. The best that could be determined was that Marcelli died of influenza pneumonia, and she was buried on the family property, which was common in Sienna.

Haroldo was a loner and lived on a couple of acres with a small farm that produced enough for him and Aylen. Haroldo did odd jobs and was particularly good at repairing farm machinery, which gave additional income for the two, but for the most part he kept to himself and was very protective of Aylen.

The first time Doc met Aylen was when Haroldo brought her into the office to receive vaccinations that were required for her to start school, and he needed a birth certificate, because all Haroldo had was what the nurse-midwife had given him when Aylen was born. When Doc reviewed it, the nurse-midwife document was enough for Haroldo to obtain a birth certificate. Doc directed him to the health department and told him to come back for the shots as soon as he had the birth certificate. A couple of months later, Haroldo and Aylen returned.

Retrospectively, Doc recalled how well-spoken Aylen was, and he was impressed with how Haroldo had done a good job teaching her the alphabet and numbers. She could easily write her name and seemed to be in overall good health. She was very shy, but that was to be expected, given how much Haroldo sheltered her.

Haroldo said to Doc on that second visit, "Doctor, I love my little Aylen very much. When her mother died, I was so depressed, and I promised myself that I would protect Aylen and give her the very best life I could. She is my happiness!"

Doc responded, "Well, Mr. Haroldo, you are doing an awesome job. Aylen is very smart for her age and should do well in school. We will need to see her more often at first to get her caught up on her immunizations. We've started the series, so she will be good to start school in August. You take care, and we'll see you both again in a few months."

The years went by, and Doc became very fond of Aylen and invited her and Haroldo to several of the community events that were sponsored by the Community Center for Youth. They two would always come, and Aylen would enjoy the community educational events. Haroldo would not interact with the parents but always kept his attention on Aylen. After the third time, Alice invited them to come to their house for dinner. Both Phillip and Aylen were just entering middle school, and Phillip thought she was the prettiest girl ever! Of course, he only told his mother that, and he made sure he never told Aylen.

There was a rumor around town that Mr. Haroldo had made a pledge in blood to kill any boy who showed any interest in Aylen. In a way, Mr. Haroldo was one of the scariest men in town; maybe it was because he said so few words and only watched others. Even at dinner, Doc noticed how Haroldo would laugh during the conversations but said very little to initiate any. That was okay, though, because the boys and Aylen always had plenty to say!

It was one of many dinners that would occur at the home of Doc and Alice with Haroldo and Aylen. In an unusual way, they became an extension of the family. After attending the First Presbyterian Church a few times, Haroldo decided that the Presbyterian Church was too culturally different for him and Aylen, so they started attending Hillside Baptist Church. But even at Hillside, they were considered different.

Aylen excelled in her studies and was graduating salutatorian of the class of 1984, and Doc knew that Phillip was very happy for both of them. Aylen was—well—like a cousin to Phillip. She had a kind and gentle spirit about her, and because Haroldo never changed, Doc could tell that Phillip never quite felt comfortable being alone with Haroldo.

The second student-patient whom Doc was so excited about in the graduating class was Sallie. Her daughter, Edna, was almost six years old now and was being raised by Sallie's mother (Diane) and father (Gerald). Bobby, Edna's daddy, left town shortly after learning that Sallie was pregnant, and it was believed that he was in New Jersey living with his maternal uncle. Sallie's brother, David, stayed in town for a year after Edna was born to help with the baby, and then he left to attend Florida State University, graduating in accounting. He had just started an accounting business as a CPA in Sienna, which appeared to be doing well.

The odds were stacked against Sallie the day she came alone to the office to see Doc. That day was hard to forget, because it was the same evening that Harry was murdered. In that twenty-four-hour period, more bad had occurred than good.

But Sallie kept pushing forward, even when she was ostracized by those in the community. At the time, things were changing for unwed teenage mothers, and New Horizons offered the opportunity for the mothers to attend school and not drop out. Sallie, with the help of her family, took advantage of the appropriate government programs to support her and Edna. It was the only time that Doc could remember this happening, and he hoped and prayed that he could witness other young teenage mothers pressing forward and receiving their education. It was hard for the teenage girls to complete a high school education alone, and support was needed by those closest to the unwed mother.

Now here Doc sat, proudly sharing the excitement of the three graduating young people—Phillip, Aylen, and Sallie—as well as many more, all kiddos whom Doc had cared for over the eighteen years. He was getting to the point where he was taking care of the children of the children! It was a good feeling, and in those short minutes of reflecting on the past, Doc decided it was well worth the sacrifices he and Alice had personally and professionally made.

All three of the graduates were going to strong colleges: Phillip to Rhodes College, Aylen to University of Florida, and Sallie to Florida State University. Doc was somewhat concerned about Aylen going to such a large university, but in the end, it might help bring her out of her introversion. She was planning to major in chemistry and then go on to medical school.

Sallie was interested in nursing and was accepted into the nursing program at Florida State University.

Out of the three, Doc was hopeful that at least one would end up in medical school, become a physician, and return to Sienna. His heart was still into the idea of building successful medical practices in Sienna. He couldn't work forever! It had already been seventeen years since he opened the practice.

Phillip gave a very impressive valedictorian speech, and Aylen followed with a very uplifting salutatorian speech. Doc whispered under his breath, "God is good all the time, and all the time, God is good."

CHAPTER 7

*"A merry heart doeth good like a medicine:
but a broken spirit drieth the bones."
(Proverbs 17:22 KJV)*

For six months, Dr. Campos made twice-monthly visits to see George Williamson. Antidepressants didn't work at all. A trail of multiple antipsychotics were administered, and finally, Prolixin seemed to work the best. Due to his limited ability to swallow, liquid Prolixin was used, and George was transitioned to the monthly injectable. ECT only gave temporary improvement, so after a couple of treatments, it was discontinued.

The Prolixin treatment allowed George to walk around, open his mouth to be fed, and to talk, although his conversation was mainly rambling to himself. After a year at the Florida State Hospital, Iona and Jethro brought him back home.

They hired a nursing assistant to watch him during the day so that Iona could have a break and leave the house to run errands and such. George began to develop a movement disorder called tardive dyskinesia from the Prolixin.

Doc and Dr. Campos continued to make house calls to George, because it seemed the right thing to do. Doc wasn't sure how Iona kept her spirits up seeing George shuffling around and mumbling words that no one could understand.

On December 1, 1984, Doc received a call around 4:00 a.m. It was Iona, screaming over the phone, "He's gone, he's gone, oh, dear Lord, my George is gone!"

When the paramedics arrived, there was nothing to be done. George had died in his sleep from a presumed heart attack. He had the most peaceful look on his face. Finally, his torment was over, and many in town would later say that "old man George" had died of a broken heart. The psychotic break was just another sign of a man who had lost the will to live after the death of his son. Life seemed quite unfair.

Jethro would continue to run the First Sienna Bank. He and his wife eventually moved back out to the homestead estate with their four children, and the house took on life again. Iona never remarried but started coming into town more and playing bridge at the club again. She started growing roses and participated in the Rose Garden Club.

Later, Jethro removed the large white cross his father had put up at the site where Harry had died. Instead, he planted a Magnolia tree on the side of the road, because it was more appropriate for a young life like Harry's that was so full of hope and promise before being untimely snuffed out.

The days passed quickly, and before Christmas Carrie contacted Doc to let him know that Ronnie, her nephew, was taking over to lead the family funeral business. She and Hemmey were relocating to Jacksonville, Florida, and he had accepted a job with the Florida Department of Law Enforcement (FDLE). The position offered a higher salary and the opportunity to move up in leadership.

"Doc, I want to thank you for all you have done to support me and Hemmey. Our lives are better because of your concern for us when we lost our children. May the Lord always bless you. I am happy, and although we don't have any children, we have each other. We decided not to try anymore to have a child. We will remain content with our nieces and nephews. Lord knows, we have enough of them to love!"

"Well, Carrie, take care of yourself, and stop by the office or house anytime you are in town. Our doors are always open to you and Hemmey. May the Lord continue to bless both of you," Doc responded.

Doc hung up the phone and said a short prayer for Carrie and Hemmey. They were a couple who endured and overcame significant losses, and only the Lord's mercy, grace, and love could have brought them through. Doc was thoroughly happy for them.

Despite that, Doc still had dreams about little Sabrina and little Hazel. He didn't think he would ever get over the losses. He merely suppressed them.

At Christmas, the house was full of excitement again because the three boys returned home from Washington DC (Steven), Charlotte, North Carolina (Marcus), and Memphis, Tennessee (Phillip). Doc's parents and Alice's parents came over as well for the Christmas Eve service at the church and stayed over for Christmas Day. It was good to have the family together again, and for once, the phone didn't ring for Doc to come to the hospital for an emergency! It truly was Christmas!

On Monday, December 31, the clinic was closed, but Doc decided to go in and catch up on some paperwork. He heard a faint knock at the side door that the staff used to enter the office. He went to the window to look out, and to his surprise they were standing there waving—Sallie and Aylen.

Doc was so happy to see both of them. He opened the door and said, "What in the world are you all doing, coming to see an old pediatrician like me on New Year's Eve?"

They laughed and started talking as he let them in the door.

Sallie started first. "Doc, you won't believe it, but I made all A's this semester! It's so awesome to be in college, and I never could have done it without your help. It was a lot of work, but I know I can make it. I think when I come out of nursing school that I'll concentrate either on pediatrics or on OB/GYN. It's just good to have a good start with all A's! My parents are excited about it too, and Edna just keeps growing. The only thing is that she treats me more like a big sister than a mother. I guess that's okay, because Momma, Daddy, and David have really been raising her. I am thankful for that."

"Well, Sallie, I am so excited to hear that. I knew you could do it. And I can tell you, the time will go by quickly. Just study first, and there is always plenty of time for fun after your work is done."

Sally nodded her head and replied, "Yes, sir. I always remember you saying that."

Doc turned to Aylen, and said, "Well, Aylen, how are things at University of Florida?"

Aylen said, "Everything is going well. I've made a few friends, and I made all A's as well! Daddy is very happy for me. I am happy too! UF has a lot of students, but it's not so bad that I can't find my way around. Overall, I like it."

Smiling, Doc said, "Well, that is so great to hear, Aylen. I knew you would do well too. Listen, I am waiting for the day when you all will come back and take over this medical community. Start to lead it into the new future it deserves! I just wonder if I can wait that long!"

They laughed, got up and shook Doc's hand, and agreed that they would stop by again after the spring semester. Doc was glad to see them and hoped they would continue to stay in touch. It was a great way to end the year. The land of opportunity was before them; they just had to continue to walk in it and perform well in college.

CHAPTER 8

"To every thing there is a season, and a time to every purpose under the heaven: . . . A time to get, and a time to lose."
(Ecclesiastes 3:1, 6 KJV)

From January through February of 1985, the clinic saw the usual rise in common cold and influenza cases. For the most part, the children recovered with just symptomatic support. By March, it seemed that the number of cases were starting to decrease, and the three doctors finally had a chance to sit down and plan for the upcoming spring and summer.

Doc started first. "Well, Maria and Arthur, I can't thank you enough for continuing to be partners with me. The practice is as busy as ever, but the number of winter infections are starting to decline. I thought it would be good for us to sit down and plan for vacations during the spring and summer. What do you all have in mind?"

Dr. Watson answered first. "Well, Steve, I wanted to wait and tell you sometime later, but I guess now is as good as ever. I've decided to move to California. Nancy wants to go back to Stanford to teach anthropology, and they have offered her a job starting in the summer. John will start high school in the fall, so this is a good time for us to make the transition. I hate to leave the practice, but Nancy has done a lot to support me, and I kind of feel like it's her time now."

Doc was stunned, as this seemed to come out of nowhere, but being the consummate professional and friend, he said, "Arthur, I am very surprised, and I wasn't at all expecting this . . ."

Dr. Campos interrupted by saying with a smile, "Arthur, just let Nancy go, and you and John stay here!"

"I know you are teasing me, Maria, and I would stay if Nancy wasn't going so far away. It's a dream job for her, so John and I will go. I think John will miss his close friends, and I sure will miss you all and the practice, the kids, and the town. It's been rewarding these last eight years to have the small-town connections and friendships."

Doc responded, "Well, Arthur, I wish you, Nancy, and John only the very best. Just write down what time you want to take off and when, so that I can work around that schedule. Maria, you do the same. Then we can make sure the clinic is covered. It's a godsend to have the Family Medicine residents here every month. It really is like having a fourth doc in the clinic, and it is rewarding to teach them too."

Dr. Campos said, "I agree. Let's just plan to each take a week off in March and April, before Arthur leaves. Then we can decide what to do after that."

The other two agreed on the schedule that would work for the next four months. Dr. Watson would leave the practice and relocate to California in late July or early August.

Before leaving the clinic that evening, Doc called Betsy into his office.

"Well, Betsy, I have some sad news. Dr. Watson is moving to California because Nancy is taking a teaching job at Stanford."

"Oh no, Doc! What will we do? It's been so nice having three docs here, and then the residents just makes it so nice with the flow and all. And then when you or the other docs go to the emergency room or hospital, the patients are still being seen in the office. It has worked out so well."

Doc tried to sound reassuring. "It will be okay, Betsy, we'll figure it out. We always do. I was just hoping to spend more time with Nathaniel before he graduates next year. Maybe there's some way I can make that happen. Let's keep the faith; something will work out."

Betsy was nodding her head. "Okay, Doc, we'll start working on the schedule, and I won't schedule any patients with Dr. Watson after mid-July. Will that work?"

"Let's make it the end of June. He can see the walk-ins and ER patients for the month of July, if he is still here. Thanks, Betsy."

"You bet, Doc. I'm just worried about you."

The next month, Doc was contacted by Tallahassee Memorial Hospital's chief operating officer. TMH was planning to build a medical office to support up to four physicians, and they wanted to know if he was interested in continuing to work with the residency program. Doc assured them that he was still interested and was enjoying teaching the physician residents who came to the clinic each month. Nothing needed to change, and he looked forward to having some young physicians in Sienna to practice full time one day. Doc strongly believed that serving as an attending in the residency program would be a good feeder for building the medical community with younger physicians who were interested in becoming part of the Sienna caregiving fabric.

When school started in August, Dr. Watson was gone, and with his departure, Dr. Campos and Doc were busier than ever. Betsy was doing her best to keep up, along with the other nurse, Samantha ("Sam"), and the two receptionists, Eva and Geraldine ("Gerri"). Doc seemed to become more tired as the weeks rolled by, and what helped him get through each day was the energy and youthfulness of the children coming into the office. They reinvigorated him each day to keep going.

One day, Betsy came rushing around the corner and ran into Doc, who was entering the corner room.

"Hey, Betsy, slow down! What's going on?" asked Doc.

"Well, Doc, you won't believe this. You know Ronnie, who owns the funeral home? Well, guess what? He has a child that he just got custody of last month, and the little boy is living with him. And he has him here for his shots to start school. I thought he didn't like us at all, Doc. He was always different, but here he is, bringing his little boy to see you! It's just great to see the families come, generation after generation! I just wanted to hurry over and let you know before you went into the room." Betsy was so excited that she gave Doc a hug.

"Well, that's good, Betsy. I'll go in and meet the little guy. What's his name?"

"He's Ronald Jr., but they call him R.J."

"Okay, that's easy to remember." Doc took a look at the chart that Betsy had handed him. In it was the birth certificate, showing that Ronald Ellis Jr. was born on May 5, 1969, in Duval County, and the mother was listed as Jessica Garvey.

"This should be interesting," Doc whispered to himself.

He opened the door and entered the room to see Ronnie, now thirty-four years old, sitting on the chair with his sixteen-year-old son sitting on the exam table.

Ronnie stood up and shook Doc's hand, saying, "It's good to see you, Doc. This is my son, Ronald Jr., but we call him R.J. It's hard to believe that you used to see me, and now you are seeing my son! I appreciate all that you do for Sienna, the children, and the families. I really do."

R.J. looked very much like his father. At age 16, he was already 6'1" and weighed only 150 pounds. His skin was much lighter than his father's, with straighter, dark-brown hair.

"Hello, R.J., it's nice to meet you."

R.J. reached out his hand and shook Doc's while he said, "It's nice to meet you too."

Ronnie started talking as Doc began to examine R.J.

"Well, Doc, I know you didn't know that I had a son. I've been going over to St. Augustine at least once a month, sometimes more often, to stay involved in R.J.'s life. His mom and I met while in mortuary school in Jacksonville. Before R.J. was born, I wanted to marry her, but she didn't want to come and live in Sienna. I had to keep my word and return to the family business. She didn't have a family business and wanted to stay in St. Augustine, where her family was from. Her father is White, but her mother is Hispanic. Well, we got married anyway, and it just didn't work out, with the distance and all. We divorced and she remarried, and now she has two other children, both girls. R.J. decided he wanted to come and live with me, play basketball at Sienna High School, and learn more about the business. He's done very well in school. Well, that's the story, Doc."

Doc responded, "I'm glad he is here, and I look forward to seeing him in a few basketball games. He is tall enough to play on the varsity team. Nathaniel is on the team as well, so I'll let him know about R.J. Right now, R.J. doesn't need anything else done on this visit. He is up-to-date on everything. Betsy will get the forms completed. It is so good to see you again, Ronnie, and R.J., it's nice to meet you. Take care, and contact me if there is anything I can help you with as you get settled into life here in Sienna."

Two hours later, the clinic was quiet, all the patients had been seen, and the nurses, receptionists, and Dr. Campos had left. Doc had already done his rounds on the newborns in the hospital, and there were no sick children on the floor to see. Dr. Campos would be on-call for the ER tonight. He should be able to make it home for dinner.

Doc thought about the visit from earlier in the day that was the highlight and joy of being a pediatrician: seeing an introverted child, such as Ronnie, grow up to be a responsible father, continue with a successful family business, and become a leader in the community. And the bonus was knowing that his son, R.J., had a chance to do the same, if not better. Maybe he could even get R.J. to be interested in the field of medicine, instead of mortuary science. It was worth a shot. He was unlikely to be successful with any of his sons following in his footsteps as a physician. Doc sighed over that thought, got up from his desk, turned off the lights, and exited the side door to drive home to have dinner with Alice and Nathaniel.

When he arrived home, dinner wasn't quite ready, and Nathaniel was out with some friends.

Doc sat on the sofa to wait for Alice to call him. While he was waiting, he drifted off to sleep.

The cute little four-year-old, Nina, was sitting on her mother's lap. She had the warmest kiddie smile, with all of her teeth intact and good dentition, as she smiled at Doc. He pulled the ophthalmoscope from the wall and shined the light first into the right eye, and then the left—it wasn't there. The red reflex in the left eye was missing.

Doc looked quickly at his note from the previous year. The red reflex was noted by him, and he knew he would not have documented it as being present, if he had not checked it and seen it. Her extraocular movements were intact in both eyes at last year's visit too. Today, the left eye was deviating and not tracking well. This was not good.

Doc turned to the mother, "Ms. Wells, have you noticed Nina running into things, or not noticing things on her left side?"

"No, Doc, I haven't noticed anything like that. What's wrong?"

"Well, I'm concerned because her eye exam is abnormal. I want to send her down to Shands in Gainesville. They can do some imaging and have the right eye doctors there to treat what I think may be a growth in the back of her eye. Let me make a few calls, and then I'll be right back."

"Is it a cancer, Doc? Is that what you mean by a growth?"

"Yes, I am concerned that it could be a cancerous growth, but we need more information. Hold tight; I'll be back in about fifteen minutes."

Doc went out and found Betsy. She placed the call to the Shands Pediatric Ophthalmology department and obtained an imaging appointment. Nina would go down in four days for imaging and see the ophthalmologist, Dr. Burns, on the same day as the imaging.

Nina's mother brought her back to see Doc months later. The tumor in her retina had been large and aggressive. Shands had performed an enucleation, and little Nina had an ocular prosthetic. Her left eyelid was drooping, and her face was asymmetric.

Doc, was shouting loudly, "No, no, don't take her eye! Don't take her eye . . . fix her face . . . fix her face . . ."

"Steve, wake up! Wake up!" It was Alice, shaking Doc to wake him up. He was having another bad dream.

The real situation with Nina was that she had the retinoblastoma in her left eye, and Shands was able to treat it with chemotherapy and surgery. Her vision was preserved, and there was never a need to remove her eye. Regular follow-ups at Shands and with Doc didn't show any return of the cancer.

CHAPTER 9

*"That the generation to come might know them,
even the children which should be born;
who should arise
and declare them to their children."
(Psalm 78:6 KJV)*

"Ten, nine, eight, seven, six, five, four, three, two, one!" The buzzer sounded, and the Sienna High School gym rocked with cheers and shouts from the basketball team members and from those in attendance. The 1986 boys' basketball team had just won the district championship for the first time in nineteen years.

Doc was immensely proud of Nathaniel, R.J., and the rest of the team. Almost every boy on the team had been a patient in the clinic off and on, and when Doc looked, he could find only one player that he couldn't remember seeing at some point in the clinic.

The team would move on to play in the state tournament, with the hopes of bringing the trophy home to Sienna.

Truth be told, Doc had almost missed the game. Dr. Campos was out ill with gastroenteritis, and one hour before the game was to start, Doc had been called by the ER to come and see a little baby that had been brought in by parents who were migrant farmers.

When Doc arrived, Javier, the four-month-old, was lying in his mother's arms, and the ER nurse had given the mother a bottle with Pedialyte in it to see if the baby would drink it.

Baby Javier was obviously malnourished, and Doc thought it was highly likely that the parents had been diluting the formula to make it last longer. He ordered the basic labs and asked the nurse to bring in some baby formula and start an IV on the little one. Given the paleness of the skin, the baby was probably anemic as well, and Doc finished the exam and talked with the parents. Javier would need to stay in the hospital for a few days, and Doc would know more as they monitored his electrolytes and responses to external stimuli. Doc wasn't sure the parents really understood what he was saying. He could speak some Spanish but wasn't excellent at it. What the parents did understand was that their baby was sick and the hospital was a place to come to for help.

Doc assumed they were not legal immigrants, and he would let the social worker figure all of that out. He needed to get to the gym before the end of the first half. He had missed enough events that the boys had been a part of, and he didn't want this to be another occasion of letting both Nathaniel and Alice down by not showing up.

The baby was stabilized, and he could check on the little one again after the game was over.

He slipped into the gym and sat down next to Alice as the clock showed ten minutes left in the first half. Sienna High was winning by four points. The final score ended up 74–77, and R.J. had scored the final shot with just two seconds left in the game to seal the win.

Doc had already arranged to pay for dinner at Jimmie's Restaurant, where the team would enjoy Jimmie's famous meatballs and spaghetti. The garlic bread was the best in the area, and Jimmie had given Doc a great price for the event. Nathaniel was pleased to have his father present for the night.

After leaving the restaurant, Doc dropped Alice off at the house and returned to the hospital to check on little Javier.

The team would go on to lose in the first round of the state playoffs, and the remaining months of the school year rolled quickly by.

* * *

The interesting thing about having children who were two years apart was that the educational events seemed to occur in pairs.

Spring graduation was upon the Hamiltons again. Nathaniel was graduating from high school, and Marcus was graduating from North Carolina State University with a degree in mathematical sciences. He had already been accepted into the master's program and would start that in the fall semester.

Doc's oldest son, Steven, had been working with Catholic social services for the homeless in DC. Through this work he learned that many of those living homeless on the streets were schizophrenic. One of the priests befriended him and placed him on a research project about housing in DC. It turned out to be a very rewarding learning experience. Father Stanley was most interested in what worked and what didn't work, as far as housing management. Now, after two years, Steven had applied to various law schools, and it was the services and experiences in Catholic Charities that really helped him get accepted into George Mason University. Steven was excited to start his law studies at George Mason.

Meanwhile, Phillip was still at Rhodes College in Memphis, and Doc was hoping that he would take the necessary prerequisites for medical school, even though he was a psychology major. Maybe at least one son would follow him into the practice of medicine.

Once again, Doc sat in the high school graduation, wondering how the time had gotten past him so quickly. His mind reflected back to 1973, when the boys were five, seven, nine, and eleven years old. They were supposed to go on vacation to Disney World because the boys hadn't been yet, and Nathaniel was old enough to walk around the theme park and go on some of the rides.

Complicating when they could leave for vacation was the fact that Doc had a nine-year-old patient, Priscilla, with the most severe form of lupus. Over the span of her short life, the disease had put her into end-stage renal failure. The limited medications available had not been able to control the destructive pattern of the antibodies attacking and destroying her kidneys. She was finally enrolled in hospice, and Doc thought she would pass away quickly. Dr. Campos hadn't joined the practice yet, so Doc couldn't leave town with Priscilla being terminal and expected to pass away at any moment.

The younger boys just couldn't understand, and every morning and every evening they would ask, "Is she dead yet? Is she dead yet?"

He would cringe every time they asked. It just sounded so callous, but they were kids and very concrete in their perspective. The vacation was delayed for a week due to the transition process from this life to the next that Priscilla experienced.

The boys were excited to leave for Disney, and the five-year-old said, "Well, she finally died, Daddy!" Doc couldn't respond; he felt sorry for the parents of Priscilla and for how much she had suffered in her nine short years. It wasn't fair for him to expect his sons to understand how their questions and comments were lacking in compassion or empathy. Only Steven Jr. and Alice seemed to understand, and for that Doc was thankful.

His reminiscences ended as the band started playing "Pomp and Circumstance," and the graduation ceremony began. Nathaniel was graduating, and the Hamiltons were becoming empty nesters. Maybe one day they would have grandchildren, and the house would have little ones running around again.

As it turned out, Steven was going to law school full time, and then he was recruited to join in advanced work related to the president's inauguration, serving as security for the diplomat from Jamaica. Later, while still going to law school, he obtained high clearance, and when the Attorney General had to fire two of the aides, his past girlfriend, who had gotten him started in security, thought of him. Consequently, as Steven graduated from law school, he already had a job offer with the Attorney General's office. He would stay there for two years and then move on with the Federal Prosecutor's office for nine years.

It only took Marcus one year to complete his masters in math, and he became interested in environmental issues. After interviewing for many jobs, he grew weary, bought a truck, and started gardening while teaching at Meredith College part time. Doc wasn't sure how Marcus could come up with so many interests and have so many creative talents! Shortly thereafter, he added in a business in swimming pool and yard services to his ventures. Most of all, Marcus didn't like stress, and he wanted to have a schedule that had the freedom of flexibility.

In October, Doc's brother, Alex, called, inviting Doc and Alice to come to his house for dinner to discuss a business idea. Alex was always thinking of ways to bring in more income. He had left Sienna for a short time and went to Ocala as the co-owner of a fertilizer company. His two girls and his wife hated living in Ocala, so after about four years, they came back to Sienna. He took over the fertilizer business that their father owned, and things had gone well since then.

Overall, the six children that Doc's parents had were doing well, and they all had college degrees. From the small town of Sienna, that was quite an accomplishment, and Doc felt like their Christian upbringing had a lot to do with their success in education. Alex had an agricultural degree from the University of Florida, and the four sisters had undergraduate and graduate degrees from Wesleyan College, with the second-to-youngest having a degree from Florida Presbyterian. Three of the sisters were in education and teachers or professors, and the oldest sister was the organist and pianist at the First Presbyterian Church.

The siblings' children were all doing well too, so really, Doc was exceptionally grateful with the blessings poured upon the family from generation to generation. Alex had always been a patient, loving, and supportive husband and father, and Sue was attentive to the needs of Alex and the two children. Nevertheless, Doc wasn't looking forward to having dinner at Alex's place, because Sue was not a good cook at all!

When they arrived, Doc and Alice could smell the meat cooking on the grill. They both smiled because it meant Alex was cooking and not Sue. They already knew what the food choices would be: barbecue ribs, chicken, baked beans, tossed salad, and sweet tea. Alex always prepared the same meal, but at least he was good with those few food choices, and it kept them from having to eat Sue's cooking.

Sue prepared the plates, and they sat down at the table on the back porch to eat. Alex took a sip of iced tea and said, "That tea sure is good. Now, Steve, I want to ask you about something—well, really, to tell you about something. You know Malcolm is still in the service, but Mr. Henry says he's thinking about coming out in the next year or so. Well, there's this idea I've had about starting a private school. What do you think?"

Doc had a puzzled look on his face and responded, "Alex, what in the world makes you think that you can start a private school here in Sienna, and what does Malcolm have to do with it, even if you did start a school?"

Alex wasn't dissuaded by the questions, "Well, see, that's what I'm saying. I figure, with his military experience, he could serve as the principal, and we could start with some of the older teachers who have retired, and maybe get some volunteers from the church. Maybe even some of the teachers from the White and Black churches would volunteer. I know you've been trying to get some young doctors to come to Sienna, and this way we could educate and train them up from elementary school through high school."

Doc took a big swallow of tea and then said, "That would be a big educational enterprise, and I don't know if there is enough interest and private income to have all of those grades in a start-up school. Have you talked to any of the retired teachers to get their thoughts? What about starting with just an after-school program to tutor math and science? That is where most of the kids have difficulties, especially as they are entering middle school."

Alex rubbed his forehead. "Well, I hadn't thought about that. I'll talk to a few of them and see what they think. Anyway, I was just trying to think of a way to help you as well as a way to make some money."

"Alex, I don't know that there is a lot of money to be made in private education. Maybe it would be better if you opened a trade school to teach young adults about the fertilizer business! That might be more profitable."

Alex laughed and said, "You know, brother, you are probably right!"

After dinner, they watched a couple of shows on TV, and then Doc and Alice headed back into town.

On the way home, Alice asked Doc, "Do you really think Alex was serious about the school? It sounded so ridiculous that I was surprised you didn't laugh out loud."

Doc chuckled and said, "Well, Alice, I thought it was an outlandish idea. Alex has no experience in education. I can appreciate that he is trying to help, but it was so far out of left field. His mentioning Malcolm gave me one thought—that I need to get out to see Mr. Henry. It's been a while since I've seen him, and I'm sure it's lonely for him out there all by himself. I'll see him sometime this weekend."

The next day, Doc arrived in the late morning to visit Mr. Henry. He was sitting outside the door on the porch in a light-blue cotton shirt with dark-blue denim overalls. The tan straw hat on his head made him look like a true farmer. In reality, Mr. Henry had not farmed in years. His main activity was volunteering at the church and working with Haroldo part time on farm equipment that the locals would bring to him.

"Mr. Henry, how are you doing? It's been a while since I've seen you." Doc shook Henry's hand and gave him a light tap on the shoulder. They both sat down in the rockers on the front porch.

"Well, Steve, I've been doing okay. I stay busy with the church duties and fixing up things that folks bring me. I still have my down days over all that's happened. It sure is good to see you. I think Malcolm is coming home for Christmas. He keeps talking about getting out of the Army. He's been in for over thirty years now. I think it's time for him to come out, don't you?"

"If he doesn't enjoy it anymore, I guess it's time," Doc responded.

"The thing is, Haroldo comes by quite a bit. He's real good at fixing things, so once in a while, I need his help. That's how he started coming by, and then he just kept coming about once a week to visit. Since his girl left for school, you know, college and all, he's been coming by more. I really enjoyed Aylen coming with him. She's a sweet girl, and I kind of treat her like a granddaughter. I do miss seeing her, but she stops by when she's in town from school. Malcolm likes her too. I don't think Malcolm is ever gonna get married. He's kind of an old man now, you know?"

Doc nodded and said, "Well, he might get married one day. You never know, when or where, but it might happen."

Doc felt sorry for Henry and the loneliness he was subject to since the death of Wilma and her family. He spent an hour or so visiting, and then he left to head over to his parents' home. They were not home, and he learned later that they were over visiting at Alex's place.

The Thanksgiving and Christmas holidays arrived quickly, and Doc closed the office for a week between Christmas and New Year's Day. On Monday, January 5, 1987, he received two surprises.

The first surprise was that Dr. Campos was retiring and moving to Puerto Rico to take care of her aging parents, who spoke only Spanish and were not willing to move outside of Puerto Rico. It was disappointing news for Doc, and he wasn't quite sure what he was going to do, but he had three months to try and figure it out. Betsy had already placed a call and left a message asking for the director of the Family Medicine program to give Doc a call at the office.

The second surprise for the day came in the afternoon. Betsy was smiling as she handed him the chart, saying, "You won't believe this, Doc, . . ." and she walked away.

Doc looked at the chart. The label on the outside read, "Malcolm Washington II, Date of Birth: 10/30/1984. Parents: Malcolm and Allie Washington."

"My, my," Doc whispered as he turned the knob on the door and entered the exam room.

Malcolm stood up when Doc entered, shook his hand, gave him a hug, and said, "Doc, thanks for seeing us. I know you are surprised. This is my wife, Allie. She's from Germany, and this is our son, Malcolm the second. We call him Andy, because his middle name is Andrew, like mine. We are moving to Sienna. I have put in thirty-two years in the Army, and that's enough. I was able to get my college degree, so I have a job to teach at the high school. We will stay with Dad until I am able to buy a house. This past year, I was stationed at Fort Hood in Texas."

"It's so good to see you, Malcolm. It's nice to meet you, Allie and Andy. This is a pleasant surprise! Let me look over Andy's vaccination record, but at first glance it seems he is all set to attend day care."

Doc examined Andy, and he was a healthy toddler with evidence of being ahead in the developmental milestones for a two-year-old. He had a fair complexion, with brownish curly hair and very light brown eyes, and he could speak contextual words in both English and German. Andy was clearly biracial in appearance, but Sienna was progressing, and with the population being mainly Black, Doc did not think he would have any problems growing up in Sienna.

Doc turned to Malcolm and said, "Mr. Henry didn't tell me that you had a family!"

Malcolm responded, "Well, I didn't tell him until we showed up at his door for Christmas! I knew he would have wanted me to leave the Army sooner than I was ready. Since we were in Germany until a year ago, I didn't think waiting one more year was going to hurt anything or anyone. Anyway, he's so excited, and he loves both Andy and Allie! He may not want us to leave the house and stay anywhere else. We'll see how it goes."

Doc said, "Oh, well that would explain it. The last time I talked to Mr. Henry was just before Thanksgiving."

Doc wished them well and was sincerely happy for Henry. Finally, he had family back in town, and his days of loneliness were ending.

CHAPTER 10

"Naked, and ye clothed me: I was sick, and ye visited me: I was in prison, and ye came unto me."
(Matthew 25:36 KJV)

Dr. Campos extended her stay in the practice until July to allow time for Doc to find another partner. Even with the extra time, it didn't help, and he had been unable to find another pediatrician to join him.

It wasn't quite doomsday, though, because there was a family practice resident, Dr. Troy Bartlett, who had rotated in the clinic and was interested in coming to Sienna. Tallahassee Memorial Hospital had started construction on a building off Highway 90 that would accommodate up to four physicians, and they had hired Dr. Bartlett as their first Family Medicine doctor to set up practice in Sienna. In the meantime, Doc had agreed to allow Dr. Bartlett to see patients in his office until the construction was completed. The arrangement would give Doc the help he needed as well as allow Dr. Bartlett time to start growing his own practice. Both sides agreed that Dr. Bartlett's patient appointments would be limited to the newborns and up to age 21. This would keep the office atmosphere still very child-friendly, and Doc was pleased to know that he would not be alone in the clinic.

Early in the month, at the regional meeting for the American Academy of Pediatrics, Dr. Soros had shown Doc a portable phone that was called a "bag phone." It was bulky but well worth the initial purchase and monthly contract with US Cellular. He could now make phone calls from the car without having to look for a pay phone while traveling. There were enough cell towers in his normal travels that the bag phone was a major upgrade in his lifestyle for taking calls. As fascinating as it was to Doc, Alice was even more excited about it. After a month of using it, Doc purchased a bag phone for Alice, and now the couple could stay in contact often while Doc was away from home, whether traveling or seeing patients in the clinic or hospital. The God-given creativity of man was astonishing to Doc.

Doc wasn't sure how time could go by so quickly, but it was now 1989, and so many unexpected things were happening!

Phillip had graduated from Rhodes College in Memphis in 1988 with a degree in psychology, and he had a job with the Veterans Administration. He had stayed over a year in Memphis with his girlfriend, Carol, who was finishing school and was from Memphis. At the same time, he started renovating a house and completed the top of the apartment over the garage first. After marrying Carol, they lived in the apartment and finished the rest of the house. By this time, Carol had completed her degree, so they sold the house and were traveling to see some of the States.

Whatever hopes Doc had for Phillip to consider going to medical school were no longer present, as it was clear he was not going to follow in his father's footsteps and become a doctor. Doc tried to hide his disappointment about it and accept the other possibilities that existed for Sienna to have a young and robust medical community. Even if Phillip had pursued a career in medicine, there was no guarantee that he would have returned to Sienna, given its small population.

Aylen and Sallie continued to visit Doc at least once a year during the Christmas breaks. Sallie had graduated from nursing school and returned to Sienna to work as a registered nurse (RN) at Sienna Memorial. She was finally able to spend more time with her daughter, Edna, and Doc was so pleased with how Sallie had continued with her education despite the earlier setback as a teenage mother.

Of course, there were some conflicts with Edna being raised mainly by Sallie's parents for the past ten years and Sallie now wanting to have a more active, ongoing role in her life, but it seemed to Doc that they were working it out as well as could be expected. Sallie had her own apartment in Sienna, but Edna still stayed with Diane and Gerald during the week and would spend time with Sallie on the weekends when she wasn't working in the hospital. Doc continued to see Edna in the clinic as needed and for the routine checkups, which he appreciated. He was still so impressed with how well things had turned out for the family. Having continuity of care with his patients was one of the greatest pleasures of being a pediatrician.

Being totally committed to her dream, Aylen spent two years at the University of Florida and was accepted early into its College of Medicine during her junior year. This made her at least two years younger than most of the other students who entered the program in 1986, and she was graduating next year with plans to pursue family medicine. Of course, Doc had hoped she would choose pediatrics, but he was still excited about the possibility that Aylen might return to Sienna to practice. As a single parent, Haroldo had done quite well with raising Aylen, and because she was of Native American descent, she had received full undergraduate and medical school scholarships. It was a major financial advantage to come out of medical school without any debt.

It was October 31, 1989, when Doc received a call from Mr. Henry, asking him to come out to the house because he wanted to discuss something with him. It was a Tuesday, and Dr. Bartlett was on call for the practice and the ER. This was just as good a day as any to head out to Mr. Henry's place.

Doc called Alice from his office, and after no answer on the house phone, he was able to reach her on the cell bag phone.

"Hey, Alice. How's it going today for you? . . . Okay, good. Well, I wanted to let you know that I'm headed out to Mr. Henry's house. I'm not sure what he wants, but whatever it is, he wants to talk in person about it. I shouldn't be long. . . . Yes, I think Malcolm and his family are still staying at the house. I don't see Henry letting them leave!" Doc chuckled as he hung up the phone.

Mr. Henry was waiting for Doc on the front porch, and he had the two customary glasses of sweet tea sitting on the side table between the two rockers. They greeted each other with half hugs and pats on the shoulders.

Henry sat down, took a swallow of tea, and said, "Doc, I appreciate you coming to see me so soon after my call. I'll get right to the point, as I know time is short for you. Well, it's been, let me see . . . eleven years, yes, that's right, eleven years since Harry, Mr. George's boy, was killed by those four Black boys, and the older of the pack got the worse sentence, as well he should have."

"Yes, sir, that's right," Doc confirmed, as Henry continued.

"Well, you know the Allen boy was the youngest and most timid and turned witness against the others, but the other three all said that Allen tried to talk them out of it and just wanted to leave and go home. We still don't know why Allen didn't just run away. I guess that's just how that peer pressure stuff works against a young mind as far as good sense goes. Anyway, I wanna ask you about your impressions of Allen. Haven't you been in contact with him through the prison ministry at your church?"

"Why, yes, I have. They have him at the Jackson County facility, and our men's prison ministry does Bible study there once a month on a Tuesday night. I go as often as I can. . . . I tell you, Allen is still a quiet fella, but he's a strong Christian and has a good understanding of the Scriptures. It seems a few of the older inmates have protected him almost like a son, and they call him "young Al," to distinguish him from an older guy with the same first name. Allen has a repentant heart over what happened and has kept up with how this affected the Williamson family. He's hoping to make parole soon." Doc stopped and drank tea from the mason jar glass.

"Well, see, Doc, that's what I wanted to talk to you about, the parole hearing that's coming up. You know his momma moved up to Jackson County and has been working in a local store there to be closer to the boy. He was her only son, you know, and she still comes to Hillside Baptist every first Sunday for service and communion. She's looking for a leader to support Allen being granted release, and his parole hearing is coming up soon. I was hoping you'd be willing to serve as one of the supporters. I know you're close to the Williamson family too, so if you don't feel comfortable doing it, I can understand that too."

There was an awkward moment of silence, and then Doc answered, "Given it's you that's asking me and that I've known the boy since he was a newborn baby, I'll do it. On one condition—that he not return to Sienna to live. I think that would be too hard for the Williamson family."

Henry smiled, gave Doc a strong handshake on the deal, and then they talked sports as they finished drinking their tea.

Later that night, Doc told Alice about the visit with Henry and his request. She thought agreeing to the request was fine, and she wanted Allen to have another chance at life outside of prison. He was thirty now, and maybe there was still time for him to have a positive and productive life outside of the penal system. Harry and George were gone, and if one life could be saved in some way from such a large tragedy, then it was worth trying.

In the State of Florida, the victim or their families can speak, and the inmate's family and supporters can speak on behalf of the inmate. It would take several additional months before Doc was notified to participate in the parole hearing on the scheduled date of April 17, 1990.

The two receptionists, Eva and Gerri; both nurses, Betsy and Sam; and Dr. Bartlett all gathered in Doc's office in the early evening of April 16, after all the patients had been seen.

Betsy started talking first. "Doc, I know I don't have to say this, but you are doing the right thing to support Allen. Why, he and those other boys made a terrible decision; we lost Harry over it, and then we lost Mr. George. There's no reason to lose another life completely to prison if we can save Allen from it. Sounds like Allen has changed and done some positive things while in that Jackson County prison. I just pray to the good Lord that Allen can get out and go on with a life that's worth living."

Gerri chimed in, "I remember when Allen was so excited to be graduating from high school. It was going to be quite an accomplishment for his momma too, with him being her only boy and all. He was able to walk across the stage, even though they killed Harry before graduation, since no arrests were made before graduation day. Anyway, I just know God is forgiving, and we should be too. You'll do a good job tomorrow, Doc. We're behind you on this."

The rest of the group nodded; they drank a toast with their coffee cups and slices of pound cake that Alice had sent, and then each departed and hoped for tomorrow to go as planned, or even better.

As a prisoner, Allen had been interviewed by the parole examiner, who was responsible for making a non-binding recommendation to the commissioners who serve on the Florida Commission on Offender Review (FCOR). Allen had told his mother that the interview lasted about twenty minutes and that he had been really nervous about it. He had been asked how he felt about the crime he had been found guilty of and what would he say to the commissioners, if given the opportunity. Based on advice from his legal counsel, Allen had also submitted a written parole plan that included his plans for housing, goals he had achieved while in prison, and goals he wanted to achieve should he be granted parole.

Within ninety days of Allen's interview, FCOR set a date for the parole hearing, which was being held in Tallahassee, so Doc left around 5:00 a.m. to make sure he had time to arrive early and find a place to park prior to the hearing at 9:00 a.m.

Doc and Allen's mother, Trina, spoke first, reading from personally prepared statements. They were given a total of only ten minutes (they took eight minutes). After they finished speaking, it was time for the victim's family to speak. No one from the Williamsons' family was there. Doc already knew that would be the case, because he had talked to Iona, Harry's mother, and the family wanted to move on with life. They didn't want a lot of publicity about the murder to influence Jethro's children, who were now growing up in Sienna. With no opposition from the victim's family, Doc felt that Allen had a good chance for parole release.

One month later, Allen received the decision of the commissioners by mail. His parole release was denied, with recommendations that he earn additional certificates for self-improvement through the available classes and obtain additional job-related certifications. Also, having job offers available at the time of his review would strengthen his parole packet. His Presumptive Parole Release Date (PPRD) was set to April 28, 1993.

Doc was disappointed, and he expected that Allen would have exhibited some signs of depression after the denial of parole release. Instead, a couple of months later, when Doc attended the prison Bible study, Allen was upbeat and said to Doc, "I want to thank you, Doc, for what you did for me at the release hearing. It just wasn't my time. I guess the Lord has more for me to learn in here before I am released. I'll learn some more skills and keep studying the Bible. Lord knows I deserve to be in here after letting Harry get killed that way. I was just in a world of confusion at that time in my life. I'm blessed to even have another chance. God bless you, Doc."

CHAPTER 11

> *"And we know that all things work together for good to them that love God, to them who are the called according to his purpose."*
> *(Romans 8:28 KJV)*

It was Friday, May 4, 1990, and Alice and Doc had arrived in Tampa, Florida, for Nathaniel's graduation from the University of South Florida. He majored in English and journalism and had found his niche as a freelance writer about a year before graduating. Nathaniel was entertaining a job offer with the Tampa Tribune, but he just wasn't sure he wanted the rigidity of a work schedule through a newspaper company.

All four sons were very unique in their perspectives and career choices, and yet there seemed to be a familiar pattern in how they were selecting what work options to pursue. It seemed to center on a work lifestyle that reduced stress and gave more autonomy over work hours. It would have been ingenuous not to recognize that it was the antithesis of how they grew up as "doctor's kids." Doc had little control over when he was called away from home or away from important family events, how and when he could take the family on vacation, or even how long they could be gone once they left town for vacation. All the sacrifices that physicians make for their patients seemed to have created dissatisfaction in Doc's sons, and it was showing in their career choices.

Admittedly, Alice was not surprised, but Doc was. It was almost as if he thought there was some genetic trait that would predispose at least one, if not two, of his sons to pursue medicine. Now it was impossible to ignore that it wasn't going to happen. There would not be a physician from Doc's next generation, and he would have to hope for a grandchild to pick up the calling. Ever the optimist, he was thankful that all four boys had graduated from college, and three out of the four had advanced degrees. Perhaps, even Nathaniel might pursue a master's degree or PhD in the future. He was the most adverse to stress, so it was no wonder that he was planning to be a freelance writer!

The years of raising the boys had rested heavily on Alice, and she had done an amazing job. It was good to enjoy the weekend with them, and even Alex and his family were able to attend the commencement. Prior to leaving Tampa, Doc and Alice went to Busch Gardens and reminisced about the first time they had taken the boys to the amusement park. Indeed, the park had grown since those early years!

The next week, back in Sienna, Betsy met Doc in the hallway between exam rooms.

"Hey, Doc, just wanted to let you know that Aylen wants to stop by and talk to you. She's home this week and staying out at her daddy's place."

"Thanks, Betsy, just tell her to stop by tomorrow. Thursdays are usually not as busy as Wednesdays. You know how it is. . . . Tell her 5:30 or so."

"You got it, Doc; will do!"

The next day, just before 5:30, Aylen knocked on the back office door. Betsy let her in, and they both hugged each other.

Aylen said, "Oh, Ms. Betsy, it's always so good to see you! You never change, and I bet the office has been really busy!"

"Don't you know it! It's always busy, and I can't wait for you to come back and help us! You are coming back, aren't you? Don't break my heart now!"

THE HEART ALWAYS KNOWS · 83

Aylen raised her hand and said, "Well, if you all will take me, I sure will consider it. I wanted to get some advice from Doc today. So we'll see."

Betsy and Aylen walked down the hallway to Doc's office. All the patients were gone for the day.

Doc stood up from his desk and walked over and gave Aylen a handshake and shoulder hug, saying, "It's always good to see you, Aylen. How are you, and how's your father?"

"All is well, Doc. I appreciate you seeing me. I wanted to give you some updates. Thank you for all the support and encouragement you've given to me over the years. You know, it's always been just me and Daddy, but you and Mrs. Hamilton, and your sons, have always treated me like family. And then you introduced us to the church, and then Daddy got more involved with the Hillside Baptist congregation; it all has just worked out so well for me."

"Well, you're welcome, Aylen and you are like family to us. I'm so proud of what you have been able to accomplish. Update me on your med school and residency."

Aylen answered, "Well, graduation is May 31 at UF, and I want you and Mrs. Hamilton to be my guests, along with Daddy, Papa H. (you know, that's Mr. Henry), and Mr. Malcolm and his wife and son. I have enough tickets that all of you can come."

"Aylen, I would be delighted to attend! It's always good to be on the UF campus, and what a momentous occasion! I am so proud of you. Why yes, we will be there!"

At that moment, there was something oddly familiar about Aylen. Her eyes and facial expressions gave him a sense of déjà vu, as if he had been in a similar situation before—but that was impossible. He pushed the thought out of his mind.

Aylen responded, "I don't know if I told you, but I decided to do family medicine, and I matched at the TMH Family Medicine Residency program. I thought about pediatrics for a long time, but I wanted to do all age groups. I hope you are not disappointed. I am planning to come back to Sienna, and I was hoping you would allow me to rotate in the clinic at some point in my training."

Without hesitation, Doc responded, "Of course you can rotate in the clinic. In fact, my clinic is part of the institutional training for pediatrics for the TMH program. There's no getting around working with me!" Doc smiled and laughed softly.

Aylen stood up while saying, "Well, that sounds awesome, and I'm so glad you had some time to talk with me. I'll send the details to you about the graduation, and I can't wait to see you soon in G'ville! See you, Doc!"

"Take care, Aylen," Doc said as he walked her to the back door of his office leading to the parking lot.

Doc was on call and had a patient to see in the ER before going home. He ended up having to admit the six-month-old for dehydration, most likely due to rotavirus. It was getting late in spring for rotavirus, but it was still possible to see it in early to mid-May.

When he arrived at home, it was after 8 p.m., and Alice had waited to have dinner with him. It was a simple yet delicious meal, with pan-seared trout, roasted potatoes, and tossed salad. Doc updated Alice on the plans for attending Aylen's graduation, and Alice confirmed that she was not aware of any other commitments they had that would prevent them from attending.

Doc continued to talk as they moved from the kitchen table to the family room.

"You know, Alice, it's been a good life for us here in Sienna. We've had some setbacks, but overall, I think it has gone quite well. I mean, who knows what would have happened with the boys if we had gone to Atlanta for me to practice in a large pediatric practice? I can't imagine being happy with that type of scenario. I've tried to build a larger multi-physician pediatric group here, but I don't think I am going to be successful. It does seem that family medicine has a place here in Sienna and holds a better chance of growing. If I can continue to partner with TMH and provide the pediatric training and experience that the family medicine residents need, that may prove to be the best solution. Meanwhile, the neonatologists and general pediatricians in Tallahassee are growing and providing the backup support that I need for the clinic here. I think this is probably the better plan to pursue. In three years, Aylen may return to Sienna, and she could join me in the office, or she could join TMH. Either way, we would have another physician who is dedicated to the town and dedicated to providing high-quality care. What do you think?"

Alice held his hand while saying, "Well, Steve, it seems that's the direction things are going, so just flow with it. I think it has a greater chance of success than trying to recruit another pediatrician to come to town—especially someone who will stay."

Several weeks later, Doc watched as Aylen walked across the stage of the UF College of Medicine auditorium to receive her medical degree. He was so very proud of her, as if she were his own daughter. He recalled the first time Haroldo had visited the clinic with Aylen so that she could have her school physical and attend elementary school. A lot had occurred since then, and who knew that her first visit to his clinic would produce a relationship this close and a medical school graduate who was planning to return to Sienna after training! It all had to be in the divine plan—providential!

While in Gainesville, Doc had a chance to follow up with several key physicians involved with the upcoming legislative session. Expanding services covered by Medicaid for children and families was still a continuous push in the state, and Doc was grateful for the support UF gave toward the various causes.

The following weekend, shortly after the Sunday service ended, Doc received a call at home from Henry.

"Hey, Doc, sorry to call you like this, but I just got a call from Trina, you know, Allen's mother."

"Yeah, yeah, is anything wrong? Is everything okay?"

"Well, no . . . Allen is dead. There was a fight among the inmates, and Allen tried to help one of the injured guys and was stabbed with a shank. It seems he was stabbed multiple times in the chest;

one stab punctured his lung, and the other stab, his heart. He was pronounced dead at Jackson County hospital."

"Oh my Lord, I'm so sorry to hear that! It's another tragedy to this saga. Thanks for calling, and I'll update the church's prison ministry about Allen. How sad this is, and poor Trina, who was hoping and waiting for him to get a parole release in three years! Of the four boys, I was hoping Allen would have a chance to turn his life around."

"I agree with that, Doc. I guess it just wasn't meant to be. We'll talk later, Doc, bye now."

The news of Allen's death hit the local newspaper. There were mixed emotions about it throughout Sienna, and it brought back memories of the great tragedy that occurred that day in 1978. The Williamson family stayed quiet about the death of Allen and would not talk to the reporters.

As Iona had told Doc, "We just want Harry and George to rest in peace and for our family to go on with life as best we can. The heartache is so deep. Nothing will bring them back, and we accept that as our reality."

Doc and Alice settled into a normal routine of being alone in the house without regular visits from the sons and enjoying the times when Doc wasn't on call. The days, weeks, and months slipped away quickly, and Doc continued to see fifty or more patients a day. He was now seeing the children of the children, and in some cases, the grandchildren! Betsy was running into children and grandchildren throughout the town—in the grocery store, in the park, you name it—and the kids from the practice seemed to be in every part of the town.

Betsy loved it, and so did the rest of the clinic staff. Doc had the most popular practice in town, and the decades of being such a giving and compassionate doctor was showing. Betsy figured that Doc could run for mayor and win if he wanted to! He was a real gentleman and a great physician, and she was proud to be his nurse all these years.

Some other doctors came to town over the next three years. Dr. Lisa Broudy was the most notable one. She had attended medical school at the University of Tennessee in Memphis and then did her general surgery residency training at the University of Rochester. She was a strong proponent for tackling health-care disparities and wanted to move to a small town to provide surgical care to an underserved community. After much research, she settled on Sienna; she met with the two hospital systems in Tallahassee, and one agreed to support her with a three-year income guarantee. Her surgical skills were applauded by her peers and attendings as superb, and she had spent several extra years in Rochester doing a fellowship in colorectal surgery.

Doc was so excited to have Dr. Broudy as a colleague, and they became close from day one. She was a tall, slim, Black female who wore her hair in a short Afro style, and she quickly gained a reputation of being articulate, quick-witted, and excellent in her diagnostic and surgical skills. Dr. Broudy was able to do surgeries on both adults and children, which made her an invaluable asset to the community.

The family medicine residents started to rotate with her, and she won community attending of the year by 1992. Aylen couldn't seem to stop talking about how much she learned when rotating with Dr. Broudy, although she would temper it some and say she was learning a lot from Doc too.

Doc almost couldn't believe his good fortune. After all those years, finally Sienna was moving into a higher level of providing local care without having to send patients to Tallahassee.

TMH added to Dr. Bartlett's office with a family medicine resident who graduated from the program in 1992, Dr. Russ Kraftt, and both Dr. Bartlett and Dr. Kraftt were assisting Doc in covering the pediatric patients when he was too overwhelmed with the clinic visits or admissions. Doc was having trouble getting families to move over to the family medicine practice. They wanted to continue to see him, and he didn't have the heart to make them go down the street to the bigger, newer, and more updated clinic!

In July 1993, Dr. Aylen Hunt returned to town and joined Doc's practice as the first Sienna-born female physician to practice in the town. Doc had been the first male physician to return.

Jethro Williamson had given the practice a low-interest business loan to remodel and provide some separation for the adult and pediatric patients as well as to support Dr. Hunt's salary for the first six months.

Doc was thrilled, and there were flyers and reporters from the newspaper and local TV station who made it a sensational event! A Black, Native American physician had become Doc's first protégé, albeit not a pediatrician.

Of course, no one was more proud of Aylen than her own father, Haroldo. If only his sweet Marcelli could know of their daughter who was a doctor, practicing in Sienna! A tear ran down Haroldo's cheek as he thought about how much he still missed Marcelli, even after all these years. He had raised Aylen alone and had done the best he could.

He had taught her to treasure the land the Creator had given to them, and she had learned the basics of farm machinery and farming. Aylen always had her own horse to ride and take care of, which had given her ongoing responsibilities at a young age.

They had made regular visits to Marcelli's grave, which was on the back edge of the Hunt property, and while Haroldo held the homesite and acreage as special, he wasn't sure that Aylen would live on the property now. He couldn't blame her for wanting to live in town, closer to the hospital and medical office. All in all, Haroldo considered himself extremely blessed and had planned to slow down and allow his employees to do more of the machinery repairs going forward. Aylen was self-sufficient now, and he could start to enjoy the land more, as had his ancestors before him.

Doc was the happiest he could recall in ten years! Aylen had caught on to the nuances of private practice very quickly. She had a natural operational and business mind, and she made changes to the office and patient flow. These changes allowed the clinic to reduce the wait time for the patients being seen by the nurses and doctors. By the end of the year, the practice was still 80 percent pediatrics, but some young families were becoming patients after their newborns were seen for the first few visits.

Dr. Broudy was organizing activities for the local Habitat for Humanity in the spring of 1996. Doc wasn't sure how she found the time for providing the surgical support for the community and the level of volunteerism too. He wanted to help her, but he had some other thoughts on his mind that he needed to resolve first.

In the three years since Aylen had joined him, the practice had grown rapidly. Dr. Aylen Hunt had a sizeable adult practice now, and there were some headwinds for the practice that couldn't be ignored. The payers were becoming more difficult to deal with, and they needed a dedicated biller and coder. The practice could afford this now, because the operating margin of the practice was the best it had ever been. They had already paid back the bank loan, and yet Doc knew it would require more money to move out of the existing space to a larger building. It just wasn't something that he wanted to do at sixty years of age.

Sienna's population was continuing to grow on the east side of town, closer to the outskirts of Tallahassee, due to the easy access to I-10. This was good because families were living in Fuswah County but had well-paying jobs in Tallahassee, with private commercial insurance. This gave the practice a healthy mix of private insurance, Medicaid, and Medicare, with a smaller portion of private self-pay.

Additionally, the Seminole tribe had land west of town, and there was political movement toward them opening an entertainment site (probably gambling, which Doc was not very pleased about).

All his sons were married, and they now had four grandchildren who visited multiple times a year. Doc was finally enjoying more of the beach condo that they had purchased decades ago at Santa Rosa beach.

All of this was weighing on his mind, and so he thought it would be best to talk it over with Aylen after they finished seeing the patients in the clinic that day.

As they were in the break area around noon, Doc said to Aylen, "Let's talk about the practice after we finish with patients today. Dr. Krafft is on call, right?"

Aylen looked at the calendar on her planner and said, "Yes, he's on call. Is everything okay?"

"Yes, all is well. I just think it would be good for us to brainstorm about what the future might look like for the practice. Financially, it's all good."

Later that evening, the two met in Doc's office with a couple of cups of coffee.

Doc started talking first. "Well, Aylen, as you can see, the practice is doing well, and we are growing with both newborns and families. That's a good thing."

Aylen nodded, "I agree, and I really enjoy the patients and being back in Sienna. I always thought I would enjoy practicing back here, and I really do. Rural medicine is challenging and rewarding."

Doc responded, "Yes, yes, we are doing so well. I think it is time to expand the space. We don't have enough room. We can make the change legally, allowing us to have a fifty-fifty partnership and build a larger clinic. We are too landlocked to expand square footage at this site."

"Doc, I don't think it's fair that you spent all these years building the practice, and then I come in and in three years become an equal partner. It doesn't seem right. I'm not sure either of us should take on the debt, but I agree we need more space. Hey, what about TMH? Maybe they would be interested?"

Doc tilted his head slightly and said, "Now that's something. What are you thinking?"

Aylen continued, "Well, they already have space for two additional doctors. What if we joined them, and maybe they would be interested in expanding to another area of town or the adjoining county? That would help to meet the growing demand, and we could continue to practice without the stress of managing the practice. It might work as an option."

Doc spoke softly, almost as if talking to himself, "Yes, yes, that's an excellent thought. So then we would become employees of TMH? Are you okay with that?

"Sure, Doc, I'm fine with it. One day, you will retire, and there is no way I would want to take on managing a practice."

"I understand. You have a good business mind, but there are so many sacrifices involved in private, solo practice. At some point, you will get married and have a family. I don't want your children to have some of the negative feelings about being a doctor that my kids had. Okay, let's spend a little time thinking about it over the next week or so. If we still think it is the best option, I'll call the chief operating officer (COO) for the TMH clinics in a couple of weeks."

"Sounds good, Doc, and I'm glad we are talking about it now, before things get too critical regarding the need for extra space."

Two weeks later, Doc made the phone call to the COO for TMH, Jason Rodriguez, and the conversation went surprisingly well. It was perfect timing, because TMH was looking to add additional doctors, but they were very interested in acquiring Doc's practice and bringing on Doc and Dr. Hunt as full-time employed physicians.

Jason even recommended that Doc consider going down to four days a week, now that he was sixty, and he wouldn't have to take ER calls at the hospital any longer, based on the medical staff bylaws. Doc agreed to share the visit volumes and financials of the office with the hospital and to have a private company complete an appraisal on the furniture, fixtures, and equipment. It would take about thirty days for the full review and analysis of the data.

Doc relayed the information to Aylen, and she seemed excited about the possible change. She was also supportive of Doc going down to four days a week. TMH would expand the clinic so that two nurse practitioners could be added over the next couple of years.

CHAPTER 12

*"And God is able to make all grace abound toward
you; that ye, always having all sufficiency in all things,
may abound to every good work."*
(2 Corinthians 9:8 KJV)

On September 1, 1996, the Sienna Herald newspaper heading read, "Dr. Steven Hamilton and Dr. Aylen Hunt join Tallahassee Memorial Hospital Practice."

The article went on to give the history of Doc and his return to Sienna in 1967 as the first, and still only, pediatrician. There were quotes from parents and previous patients on the kindness and great care they had received from Doc. Dr. Aylen Hunt was hailed as the first Sienna-born family medicine physician to return to Sienna, and much attention was given to how her father, Haroldo, had raised her alone after the death of her mother when she was a toddler.

When Aylen went to visit her father for Labor Day, he was quite disturbed with all the publicity. He wanted Aylen to continue to do well in her career, but he didn't want any attention placed on himself. They spent a couple of hours riding the horses, and then Aylen drove them over to the Washingtons' for a Labor Day cookout.

When they arrived, Malcolm greeted them with his usual warm smile and genuine hug, while saying, "Welcome, welcome! I sure hope you two are hungry, 'cause you know how Papa is—he wants me to cook like army soldiers are coming to dinner! We've got a few church folks coming over, and then it's just family. Oh, and there's a new teacher from the school I want you to meet too."

Aylen responded, "Oh, okay. I didn't realize we had a new teacher at the high school."

"Yeah, he hasn't been at the school very long. He replaced the English teacher, Ms. Frenk, who abruptly retired and moved out of state to be with her grandchildren in Alabama. His name is Arturo Medina, but he goes by Art."

"Oh, so he is Hispanic?" Aylen asked.

"Yep, his parents were from Mexico, but he grew up in El Paso, Texas, so he is bilingual, which is good. It will help as he teaches the Mexican migrant children English. It's one of the reasons he chose Sienna. It's hard to believe that we have kids in high school who still struggle communicating in English."

Henry walked up as Malcolm finished talking and greeted Haroldo and Aylen. "Well, well, here is the rest of the family. How ya' doing, Haroldo? And what about you, my little Dr. Hunt?"

Haroldo said, "Well, we're doing pretty good. It's always good when Aylen can break away and come visit us out in the countryside."

Henry nodded, "Yes, sir! I agree with that! And I have my grandson, Andy, out here playing. He's growing up so fast, and he'll be eleven in October. Almost ready to start learning how to drive some farm equipment! I had given up on any grandchildren, but it is nice to know that Malcolm finally came through with at least one child! Why, he's sixty years old now. Don't let him know I told you!" Henry let out a loud laugh.

Aylen was amazed at how well Papa H. was doing. She figured he had to be close to eighty if Malcolm was sixty, but he didn't act or look that age. With Malcolm returning to town, Papa H. had gained new energy and excitement. It was interesting to see the dramatic change that occurred now that he had Malcolm, Allie, and Andy staying at the homestead. They had built a larger house on the grounds and made a covered breezeway so that Papa H. could cross over to see them without getting in the rain. Allie was working at the bank as one of the tellers and seemed to enjoy it. Aylen's thoughts were interrupted by more cars pulling up as some of the church members arrived. She stood up to greet them; she knew all of them except one, and that was because he wasn't a church member at all.

Malcolm reached him first and said, "Hello, Art, so glad you could make it. Come on over; I've got someone I want you to meet. She's part of the family."

Malcolm walked over to Aylen with Art. "Art, this is Dr. Aylen Hunt. Dr. Hunt, this is Mr. Arturo Medina. You can call him Art."

Aylen shook Art's hand and said, "You can call me Aylen."

Art returned the handshake and said, "I will only call you Aylen in this type of setting; otherwise, it is Dr. Hunt. You deserve to be called that. You earned the degree and did the training."

Aylen smiled. He had a pleasant accent and was very well spoken. He was about 5'10", with an almost bronze undertone and dark black hair. His face was almond shaped, and his physique was slim but muscular.

Art couldn't believe it. Malcolm had spoken very positively about Aylen, but he had not told him how pretty she was! The photo in the newspaper didn't do her justice. She was downright beautiful and didn't seem at all uppity, as some female professionals could be. And on top of that, she was a doctor. He probably didn't stand a chance to date her, but that wasn't going to stop him from trying.

As usual, the food was great and the socializing was exciting, with a couple of card tables going and the teenagers playing basketball on the driveway at Malcolm's place.

As things were winding down, Art saw Aylen standing up as if she were leaving. He had left the card table about thirty minutes before, because he wanted to be in position to ask for her number. He walked quickly over to her before Haroldo could reach her. "Aylen, I hope you will not find this request presumptuous, but may I have your phone number? I would like to take you to lunch sometime when you have an hour or so to talk."

Aylen thought to herself, "What took you so long?"

Instead, she said to Art, "Okay, but you don't have anything to write with."

Art replied, "I have an excellent memory, just tell it to me, and I'll remember it."

Aylen smiled and gave him her cell number, expecting that he would probably not remember it correctly.

She had a friend in the sheriff's office whom she would ask to research Art to make sure he didn't have any negative things in his past. That would be important before having lunch with him. A few days later, she learned that Art's past was unremarkable. He was "clean."

As 1996 came to a close, Doc was enjoying the reduced schedule of four days a week and not being on call for the emergency room any longer. Drs. Hunt, Krafft, and Bartlett were doing well in the TMH practice. Doc had been able to sell the practice building to an insurance company for a nice profit, although he wanted to keep it as medical space. Dr. Broudy had been interested in it, but it was more space than she needed.

Doc joined Dr. Broudy in the Habitat for Humanity project, and they were able to get the TMH residents and the office staff to help as well. She was also doing some volunteering at the homeless shelter clinic and doing minor procedures under local anesthesia. This was actually very good, because so many of the homeless had problems with abscesses that needed incision and drainage.

Doc was spending more time with his parents, as they were aging and needed more help with things out at the homestead. Alex was very involved with helping them, too, since he was working only part time overseeing the fertilizer business.

The annual Thanksgiving parade continued to occur, but the Hamiltons no longer had a major part in arranging it and supporting it. The responsibility had been taken over by Fuswah County, with First Sienna Bank as the main sponsor still. There were other businesses supporting the parade as well, and there was still a float in honor of the Wilma W. Hinson Nursing Scholarship.

At the New Year's Eve service at church, Doc thought about how blessed he, Alice, and the rest of the family were. Sure, things could have been better in some areas, and maybe he could have done things a little differently. He had spent decades taking care of the children in the community. That was the right thing to do. That was his calling. He had prayed, and he would continue to pray and ask the Lord for help and guidance. There were times when he wondered if he had sacrificed too much and neglected the boys. Alice always reassured him that he was a supporting and loving father. Still, he wanted to make sure he confessed to any sins he may have committed by omission or commission. He wanted to be right with the Lord, justified by faith, and reconciled by grace. All of this and so much more flooded his mind as the choir sang and the old year ended and the new year began.

Aylen had accepted the lunch invitation from Art, and she was finally able to break away in the first week of October to go. Now as the year came to an end, they had gone out to dinner a few times, and Aylen had invited him out to the house for dinner with her and Haroldo. Aylen had asked her father what he thought about Art.

Haroldo had said he thought Art was a nice guy, and Aylen was not surprised that her father held back on giving full approval, since by nature he was very protective of her. At this point, Aylen wondered if her father would ever willingly give his approval for her to marry anyone. After all, she was almost thirty-one years old, and at some point she wanted to marry the right person and have children and a family of her own.

She decided to take a chance and go to Tallahassee with him for New Year's Eve to the Bradfordville Blues Club. She played it safe by inviting her friend Frederica, and Frederica's husband, Zachary, to go with them. They would stay at their home in Tallahassee after the event.

The club was located on the far northeast side of Tallahassee, off a small dirt road. Frederica and Zachary had been to the club a few times and knew how to get there, so Aylen was very glad that she had asked them to go with her and Art. The entertainment was excellent, and it was a memorable way to bring in the new year.

On New Year's Day while traveling back to Sienna, Art and Aylen talked about many things—politics, religion, what they thought was important for healthy relationships, and sustainable marriages, and the list went on and on.

When they arrived back in Sienna, Art pulled into Aylen's driveway, got her suitcase out of the trunk, and opened the car door for her to get out. He took her hand, she stood up, and as she did he gently pulled her close to him and kissed her. It was a long, intimate kiss, and then they walked to the front door. As she turned on the lights to the living room, he waited at the door and asked her if they could meet for dinner the next day at his place. She said yes and closed the door. Aylen felt weak in the knees and had to sit down. Maybe this was love? Was she falling in love with this guy from El Paso?

By July 1997, the romance between Art and Aylen was going perfectly. In August, they had flown to El Paso for Aylen to meet his parents, two brothers, and sisters. It all went well, and Aylen had enjoyed the visit. The family didn't seem to mind that she couldn't speak Spanish. She was slowly learning from Art, but she was nowhere close to being fluent. On the second night of their visit, Art's parents had spoken to him alone after Aylen had retired for the night. They said that they really liked Aylen, and although she wasn't Hispanic, they thought he was making the right choice with her.

As they were flying back from El Paso, Art knew what he needed to do—there was no way he was going to let Aylen get away from him. Her father, Mr. Hunt, was a problem. Aylen was his only child, and his wife had died when Aylen was very young. Haroldo was not showing any signs of allowing Aylen to leave him and get married.

It was really quite selfish of him, in Art's mind. He would give him a call and set up some time for them to talk.

On the evening of Monday, August 11, Art called Haroldo's home number. When Haroldo answered, Art's mouth went dry.

"Hello?" Haroldo said.

"Hello, Mr. Hunt, this is Art Medina."

"Hello, Art, how are you doing? How was the trip to El Paso?"

Art took a sip of water, "Oh, it was a really good trip. Thanks for asking. Is it possible that you would have time to talk to me in person this week, without Aylen around?"

There was an awkward moment of silence, and then Haroldo said, "I guess so. Let me see... how does Thursday sound? Say about 6:30 in the evening. Will that work?"

Art responded, "Yes, Mr. Hunt, that will work just fine, and thank you. I'll see you then."

Haroldo smiled as he hung up the phone and mumbled to himself, "He sure was nervous..."

On Thursday, when Art arrived at the house, Haroldo welcomed him with a smile and handshake, saying, "Come on in, Art. I've got some chicken and fries that I picked up from Lindy's, and a couple of beers. Do you drink beer?"

"Sure, Mr. Hunt, that will be fine, thank you."

Haroldo waved him to the dining room table and said, "Well, what's on your mind? Let's say grace first."

Haroldo prayed, and then he passed a box of Lindy's fried chicken to Art and opened the one sitting in front of him.

They both took a couple of bites and a sip of the Budweiser beer. Art was thankful for the beer. Maybe it would help calm his nerves.

"Well, Mr. Hunt, I wanted to talk to you about Aylen."

"What about Aylen?"

"Well, I was wondering... well, I wanted to ask your permission to marry her.... I love her, and I give you my word that I will honor her and treat her right."

Haroldo kept eating and looking at Art. It was almost as if Art wasn't there and as if he had not said a word or asked the question.

After what seemed like eternity to Art, Haroldo said in a quiet voice, "I was wondering when, or if, you would ask. At least I know you come from a good family upbringing by coming here to ask. Aylen is my love and my only child. You know that. When her momma died, I promised the Lord I would take care of her for as long as I lived. I don't want her to be alone when I die, and my time is sure enough sooner than hers. At least, I pray so. You seem to be a good guy, Art, and I can't deny my daughter the happiness that I had with her momma. I pray that she will be as happy with you as I was with her momma. A day doesn't go by that I don't miss my Marcelli. You have my permission to marry my Aylen."

Haroldo reached across the table and shook Art's hand, which was cold and clammy.

"Relax, Art, I'm not going to shoot you! Let's finish dinner, and then we'll take a walk out to the barn and I'll show you Aylen's horse."

Art was relieved and was able to finish eating the chicken and drinking the beer. The evening turned out much better than he had expected.

Since Sienna was such a small town, Art went to Tallahassee the next week and bought an engagement ring from Helzberg Diamonds. Frederica had helped by going shopping with Aylen a month before and finding out her ring size. Everything was in place for him to pop the question, and two weeks later, while eating dinner at their favorite Chinese restaurant, Art asked Aylen to marry him. With tears in her eyes, she said yes.

A year later, they were married at Hillside Baptist Church with a small gathering of family and friends, including the clinic staff, and of course, Doc and Alice.

CHAPTER 13

"For I know the thoughts that I think toward you, saith the Lord, thoughts of peace, and not of evil, to give you an expected end."
(Jeremiah 29:11 KJV)

The next three years went by quickly, and by 2001, it was obvious to Doc that it was really time for him to retire. He thought he could practice for another few years, but the practice wanted to implement an electronic medical record (EMR). An electronic practice management system had been in place for a year and now it was time to integrate the EMR component.

Doc went through the training. Sitting there in the last class, with a headache and blurred eyes from the strain of staring at the monitor for hours, he knew it was time to retire and let the younger doctors continue with the practice.

He wanted to talk to Aylen first, before discussing it with Jason, the COO. Despite being married for three years, she and Art had not been able to have a child yet. Doc reassured them not to stress about it and that in due time Aylen would conceive.

Later in the afternoon, the two were able to talk in Doc's office.

"Aylen, you know I'm not very good at the computer stuff. I'm just too old to retain the information and feel comfortable documenting a patient visit with it."

Aylen nodded her head, saying, "Yes, it will be very different, and I can understand your hesitancy. We could get some help for you, like a scribe, to put the information in."

Doc was shaking his head. "No, no, Aylen. I don't think that is the way I should do this. I think it is time . . . it is time for me to retire. I've put in over thirty-four years practicing in Sienna, and that doesn't count the years I was in the Army. It's time; it truly is time."

Aylen nodded in affirmation and said, "I understand, Doc. I'll miss you, but you deserve to be happy and to retire while you can still enjoy life and enjoy Mrs. Alice, your sons, and the grandchildren. I won't say anything, and I'll wait for you to tell others. Let me know how I can support you as you transition into retirement."

"Thanks, Aylen. I'll let you know. I'll stay for at least four months to help with the transfer of patients. It will take some time to do that."

Later at home, Doc confirmed with Alice that they both were in agreement about him retiring. Alice was supportive and seemed relieved that he had come to the decision with just a few conversations between the two of them over the last couple of weeks. As he lie in the bed, trying to fall asleep, he reflected back on his conversation with Aylen. There were times when she reminded him of someone else; he just couldn't quite figure out who. He was almost certain that her mannerisms and facial expressions were similar to someone from his distant past. He wondered about it off and on, but he just couldn't recall who it could be.

The next day, Doc placed a call to Jason, the COO. They talked and agreed that two months would be enough time to transition, and if needed, it could be extended to four months.

The day would end with Haroldo coming to the office to see Dr. Bartlett for weakness. After a history and physical exam, Dr. Bartlett determined that the weak feeling only occurred with exertion and while carrying heavy objects. A resting EKG showed changes of an old myocardial infarction (heart attack). Since his symptoms were stable, Dr. Bartlett and Aylen agreed that she would take him the following day to see the cardiologist in Tallahassee.

Unsurprisingly, the visit to the cardiologist, Dr. Jeffers, resulted in Haroldo being admitted to TMH for a cardiac catheterization. The results showed severe triple vessel disease, and he would need coronary artery bypass grafts (CABG) to the three stenotic vessels. Aylen remained in Tallahassee, and Art joined her later in the evening.

Haroldo entered the operating room at 7:04 a.m., and the surgery was going well until he went into cardiac arrest. Despite all aggressive measures by the surgeons, anesthesiologist, and cardiac team, the doctors were not able to restore a viable rhythm, and after forty-five minutes of attempting to save Haroldo, he was pronounced dead. When Dr. Jeffers went to the waiting room to talk to Aylen and Art, it was one of the most difficult discussions he had ever done.

"Dr. Hunt, I'm so sorry. It happened so quickly. The surgery was going well, but . . ."

Aylen interrupted, "What are you saying? It was going well; what happened?"

Dr. Jeffers continued, "Well, quite unexpectantly, your father went into cardiac arrest. We worked on him for forty-five minutes, but we were unable to restore a rhythm. I am so very sorry, but Mr. Hunt has died."

Aylen collapsed into Art's arms and sobbed.

Three days later, on Saturday, Aylen asked Doc to meet her and Art at the house. She wanted to look through the chest locker that her father said contained information she would need if anything ever happened to him. He wanted to be buried beside her mother on the back of the property, but on the right side, with Marcelli's grave on his left. He had said it enough times that Aylen didn't need to look for those instructions.

As they pored through the contents, there were old, faded photos of Marcelli. There were no photos of Aylen until she started school. Doc noticed there seemed to be what looked like the corner of a brown envelope sticking out from underneath the very bottom panel of the trunk locker.

Doc said to Art, "Can you bring me a butter knife? I think there is some kind of document under the bottom inner panel."

With care, Doc was able to lift the inner panel and pull the envelope out. He handed it to Aylen.

"Hmm, I wonder what this is? That's Daddy's handwriting on the outside, and it says, 'Open only after the death of me, Haroldo Hunt.'"

Aylen sat down on the sofa, with Art next to her and Doc sitting on the love seat across from them.

It was a faded, two-page, handwritten letter on lined paper.

Dear, sweet, Aylen, if you are reading this, then I am dead. I want you to know that I love you and always will. Your momma died a few months after giving birth. I was so sad. Then something worse happened; I think the first Aylen got the same sickness, and I tried to take care of her. I was afraid of doctors. I believed in the herbs from the land. She didn't make it, and I buried her next to her momma. Weeks later, I was riding my horse in the night, and there you were—a gift from the Lord. I don't know how you made it into the deep woods or how a bear or something didn't eat you. I put you on my horse and brought you home. You were my second Aylen. I never told anyone, and I hope you will forgive me. I was so sad and lonely with losing Marcelli and the first Aylen; I just couldn't lose you, too, my gift from God. I think you had some kind of memory loss. You couldn't tell me your name, and I think you were maybe two. I was a loner and lived off the land. It wasn't until you got older that I started the machinery business to give you a better life. Talk with Doc, if he is still alive. He might know more, since he takes care of kids. Please forgive me, and promise me you will love me always, as I have always loved you, my daughter. I leave you with all of my possessions and all of my love.

Daddy (Haroldo Hunt)

The three sat in silence and were speechless. Aylen started to cry and said to Doc, "What does this mean? The first Aylen, the second Aylen? What, am I not Daddy's real daughter? How did I get in the woods? What in the world? Doc, what do you know?"

Art looked bewildered.

Doc knew the truth in his heart. It was what had been nudging him all these years. Why, it had been right before him, and he couldn't bring himself to believe what his heart was telling him. Aylen's hazel eyes and facial expressions solidified it. Aylen, her mannerisms—why, it was like Wilma's! But how?

Doc softly started to explain. "Aylen, back in 1968, Wilma, Mr. Henry's daughter, was married and had three children. A son and two twin daughters. They left in the middle of the night to go to her in-laws in North Carolina, and somehow, Larry, her husband, lost control of the car. They went over the embankment, and the car burst into flames. Everything was destroyed, and the bodies were severely burned beyond recognition. I think you somehow were thrown from the car, survived, and wandered into the woods. There was no way to even guess that one of the twins had survived."

Aylen was in disbelief. "Do you mean to tell me that Daddy didn't know I was maybe Papa H's grandchild? How could he not know?"

Doc was trying to make sense of it. "Well, your daddy was a loner and really almost a hermit. He didn't read the papers or interact much with Sienna folks. He probably didn't even know that Wilma had three kids, two of which were twins. He didn't start to socialize until you were just about to start school. When he brought you in to see me, he was able to obtain a birth certificate, which he received from the county, based on what the midwife had written down on paper. That's how things were back then. I didn't even know his baby had died. He kept it from everyone, and since no one visited, there was no reason to be suspicious. He would not have known what Wilma was like, or her children."

Art finally spoke up. "Well, this is a lot to take in. What should we do?"

Aylen responded, "For now, let's keep it between the three of us. I don't know what to do right now. No wonder I felt like family with Malcolm; he's my uncle? And then Papa H., he's really my grandfather. Lord, have mercy! Yes, give me some time to process it all. Can you all swear to secrecy until I can decide how I want to handle this? One day, I will tell the Washingtons, but I want my daddy's memory to be a good one, and I want to bury him in peace. In my heart, he is still my father."

Doc and Art nodded in agreement.

EPILOGUE

Two years later, Doc was in full retirement and enjoying it.

Dr. Aylen Hunt and Art Medina were finally successful with starting a family. They had twin sons (twins run in the Washington family) and moved out to the Hunt homestead, which placed them closer to the Washingtons, allowing Aylen to continue to care for the family burial site. She continued to call Haroldo her daddy, and she harbored no ill feelings for what he had done. He had raised her as best as he could, given what he believed was right in his heart.

The Washingtons came over two weeks later to visit the Hunts and welcome the twins. And then, over glasses of sweet tea, Aylen read the letter and told the story of what she and Doc believed was the truth, based on the timing of the accident.

Henry and Malcolm were understandably shocked and in disbelief, but the more they talked to Aylen and started accepting what had always been right in front of them, the more sense it made. Aylen had the hazel eyes and mannerisms so reminiscent of Wilma. It was almost inconceivable that they had not reasoned it out before. The visit ended without any anger or remorse—just relief that one of the five family members had actually survived. It was a true miracle of the Lord!

It would take six months before Aylen would do DNA testing, which confirmed that she was a member of the Washington family. The grave of Aylen—Haroldo's biological daughter—was not exhumed, and it was assumed she was laid to rest on the left side of Marcelli's grave. Since there was no way to know if Aylen was actually Carmen or Crystal, the Washingtons left the five named graves as they were: Wilma, Larry, Christopher, Carmen, and Crystal.

Dr. Aylen Hunt changed her name legally to Dr. Aylen W. H. Medina.

REFERENCES

1. King James Bible (1769). King James Bible Online. https://www.kingjamesbibleonline.org/ (accessed September 20, 2022).
2. Center for Medicare and Medicaid Services. "Key Milestones in Medicare and Medicaid History, Selected Years: 1965–2003." *Health Care Financing Review*, vol. 27, no. 2 (Winter 2005–2006): 1–3, https://www.cms.gov/Research-Statistics-Data-and-Systems/Research/HealthCareFinancingReview/Downloads/05-06Winpg1.pdf# (accessed September 20, 2022).
3. Oliveira, Victor, Elizabeth Racine, Jennifer Olmstead, and Linda M. Ghelfi. *The WIC Program: Background, Trends, and Issues* (Washington DC: Economic Research Service/USDA, 2002), 7–12, https://www.ers.usda.gov/webdocs/publications/46648/15834_fanrr27c_1_.pdf?v=41063 (accessed September 20, 2022).

ABOUT THE AUTHOR

Estrellita Howard Redmon, MD, MBA, FACP, was born in Tallahassee, Florida. At the age of 12, she announced that she wanted to be a doctor, and at 16, she enrolled at Florida A&M University. She earned a bachelor's degree in pharmacy, followed by a doctor of medicine degree from the University of Florida in 1986. She completed her residency training in internal medicine in Roanoke, VA (now Virginia Tech Carilion), and later returned to the University of Florida for a master's degree in business administration. Dr. Redmon is board-certified in internal medicine and health care quality management and is a fellow in the American College of Physicians. Her career includes over twenty-five years as a practicing physician and over twenty years as a physician executive. Currently, she is the Chief Clinical Officer for Ascension Florida & Gulf Coast. The health system operates ten hospitals and more than two hundred other sites of care, employing more than thirteen thousand associates and approximately nine hundred physicians. Dr. Redmon is responsible for the clinical performance across the continuum of care, including growth and development of systems of care. She is the author of *Victors Over Leukemia*, a book in which she shares her story through the eyes of her son Victor, his family, and his friends. "Dr. E" enjoys traveling with her husband, Gregory, spending time with her children and grandchildren, writing, reading, and playing the piano.

CPSIA information can be obtained
at www.ICGtesting.com
Printed in the USA
BVHW050715220223
658986BV00022B/114/J